THE BRIDES OF BELLA LUCIA
A family torn apart by secrets, reunited by marriage

When William Valentine returned from the war, as a
testament to his love for his beautiful Italian wife, Lucia,
he opened the first Bella Lucia restaurant in London.
The future looked bright, and William had,
he thought, the perfect family.

Now William is nearly ninety, and not long for this world,
but he has three top London restaurants with prime spots
throughout Knightsbridge and the West End. He has two
sons, John and Robert, and grown-up grandchildren on
both sides of the Atlantic who are poised to take this
small gastronomic success story into the
twenty-first century.

But when William dies, and the family fights to control
the destiny of the Bella Lucia business, they discover a
multitude of long-buried secrets, scandals, the threat of
financial ruin and, ultimately, two great loves they hadn't
even dreamed of: the love of a lifelong partner,
and the love of a family reunited.

Read the first two books of this compelling new
miniseries, and meet twin sisters Rachel Valentine, in
Having the Frenchman's Baby
by Rebecca Winters,
and Rebecca Valentine, in *Co*
by Patricia

*Available this month from

D1495260

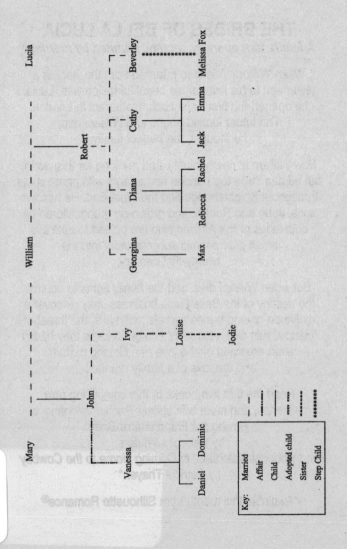

HAVING THE
FRENCHMAN'S BABY

Rebecca Winters

The Brides of Bella Lucia

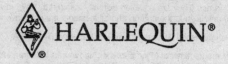

HARLEQUIN®

TORONTO • NEW YORK • LONDON
AMSTERDAM • PARIS • SYDNEY • HAMBURG
STOCKHOLM • ATHENS • TOKYO • MILAN • MADRID
PRAGUE • WARSAW • BUDAPEST • AUCKLAND

Special thanks and acknowledgment are given to
Rebecca Winters for her contribution to
THE BRIDES OF BELLA LUCIA series.

ISBN-13: 978-0-373-03904-3
ISBN-10:   0-373-03904-2

HAVING THE FRENCHMAN'S BABY

First North American Publication 2006.

www.eHarlequin.com

Printed in U.S.A.

THE BRIDES OF BELLA LUCIA
A family torn apart by secrets, reunited by marriage

**There's double the excitement in August—
meet twins Rebecca and Rachel Valentine**

Having the Frenchman's Baby—Rebecca Winters
Coming Home to the Cowboy—Patricia Thayer
(available from Silhouette Romance®)

**Then join Emma Valentine as she gets
a royal welcome in September**

The Rebel Prince—Raye Morgan

**Take a trip to the Outback and meet
Jodie this October**

Wanted: Outback Wife—Ally Blake

**On cold November nights catch up with
newcomer Daniel Valentine**

Married Under the Mistletoe—Linda Goodnight

**Snuggle up with sexy Jack Valentine
over Christmas**

Crazy about the Boss—Teresa Southwick

**In the New Year join Melissa as she
heads off to a desert kingdom**

The Nanny and the Sheikh—Barbara McMahon

**And don't miss the thrilling end to the
Valentine saga in February**

The Valentine Bride—Liz Fielding

**All forthcoming titles are available from
Harlequin Romance. This month, look out for**
Coming Home to the Cowboy by Patricia Thayer
in Silhouette Romance®.

This book is dedicated to Kim,
who has always believed in me and my ideas.
Everyone should be so lucky.

CHAPTER ONE

WHEN Rachel saw a silver Maserati careen around the bend of the narrow road and head straight for her, she yanked the steering wheel to the right, praying to avoid a collision.

To her shock, the dark-haired, Italian-looking driver slowed down and waved, as if to thank her for getting out of his way.

"You lunatic!" she shouted at him, and received a white smile for her effort before he cruised on.

Craning her neck out the window, she cried, "Lunatic!" But he'd sped up again and was out of sight before she could get her rental car started again.

The incident had left her so weak, it took a minute before she felt composed enough to continue on.

Within five minutes she arrived in the little town of Thann, France, and found the hotel where she would be staying for the night.

Before she freshened up and went out again, she had an important call to make. But the fear of her twin sister's rejection always put a knot in her stomach.

Their estrangement had gone on for too many years. It was a tragic situation Rachel wanted to fix if she could find the courage. Maybe this phone call could be the first step.

Yesterday was the anniversary of their mother's death. Normally Rachel would have flown to New York to put flowers on the grave, but this year her work prevented it.

To her relief the sexton at the cemetery agreed to accept the florist's delivery and place the flowers against the headstone.

If Rebecca had been able to visit the cemetery, she could tell Rachel if she'd seen the flowers. After six rings she heard, "Rachel?"

So her sister was in New York...

"Hello, Rebecca." She swallowed hard. "I wasn't sure if I would even be able to reach you."

"I've been in Wyoming, and only came here briefly on business. What is it?"

"H-how are you?"

"I'm okay." Was her twin's voice shaking too? Or had Rachel just imagined it. "And you?"

"I'm okay too." She bit her lip. This wasn't going well. It never went well. "By any chance did you notice some flowers on Mother's grave yesterday?"

"If you mean the potted rose tree, then yes."

"Oh, good."

After a tension-filled silence, "Is that all you wanted to know?"

Rachel clutched the receiver tighter. No...it wasn't all, but she didn't know where to begin.

"Look, Rachel, I'm in kind of a hurry and have to go."

She nodded. "So do I."

"Where are you?" Rebecca asked at the last second.

"France."

"Then I guess I should say *au revoir.*"

Tears stung her eyes. "Goodbye, Rebecca."

After her harrowing ordeal on the road a half-hour ago, this pain was all she needed.

Wiping her eyes, she got up to wash her face. Once she felt a little calmer, she went down to the front desk.

"Could you please tell me which vineyard is the best in the area?"

Without hesitation the concierge said, "That would be the Domaine Chartier et Fils, *mademoiselle.*

"If you take the road west from the town center and follow it three miles, you will come upon a fifteenth-century convent which has been owned by the Chartier family for generations. You can't miss it."

Rachel thanked him and went out to her car parked on one of the quaint side streets.

Thousands of tourists flocked to Alsace, the north-eastern province of France bordering Germany and Switzerland. Now that it was June, she'd had trouble finding a place to squeeze in.

After putting her black attaché case in the front passenger seat, she slid behind the wheel. But she wasn't quick enough to prevent a couple of guys from enjoying the view of her long, elegant legs. The skirt of her white business suit had ridden up her thighs.

Ignoring their interested gaze, she leaned over to close the door. The action caused her dark, glossy hair to swish against her shoulders. Quickly she started the car and pulled into the narrow street.

She'd passed through the town center a little while ago, having driven a portion of the village-studded wine route from Colmar, a city forty-five minutes from Thann.

Blessed with a good sense of direction, she soon found herself traveling to the outskirts past Hansel and Gretel houses whose window-boxes overflowed with geraniums and other summer flowers.

Instead of the rain she'd left in the UK just over a week ago, a glorious noonday sun shone down. The rays caused a dappled effect as they penetrated the lush green foliage of the manicured landscape.

If it hadn't been for that menace who'd run her off the road, the day would have been idyllic.

Still bristling over his cavalier attitude, she eventually reached the edge of the town and rounded a curve where she discovered herself flanked on both sides by rows of tall grape vines. She followed the healthy-looking vineyard up the slope.

In the distance she spied a magnificent structure reigning over the checkerboard plots of vineyards the French called *terroirs*.

A gasp of wonder escaped her throat, prompting her to slow down so she could absorb her fairy-tale-like surroundings.

She marveled at the slightly pinkish cast to its stone walls. Any second now she expected to see Rapunzel at one of the arched windows, and the handsome prince below, begging her to let down her golden hair so he could climb up to her.

Since Rachel's early-morning flight from Bordeaux, located

on the Atlantic seaboard, such fanciful thoughts seemed part of her experience.

She'd traveled to many beautiful places in Europe on restaurant business with her father and grandfather. But this was the first time she'd felt an instant bonding to a special spot of earth. Her feelings seemed to go far beyond the physical.

In her heart she thought, I could live here for ever.

She slowed down and pulled to a stop to snap a few pictures with her digital camera before moving on.

While she did business in Alsace, she would look into buying a little house with a tiny plot of vines she could use for a retreat. One day years from now she would retire here and write her own book on wines.

Bread might be the "staff of life", but to her mind the grape vine produced the "magic of life".

It wasn't just the final product to be consumed with or without a fine meal—Rachel loved the whole fascinating process, starting with the soil, whose amalgam of elements combined with the right amounts of sun and rain to produce a unique grape that could be turned into a superb wine.

Her sensations of delight mixed with reverence continued to grow even stronger as she followed the signs that led her to an exquisite rose garden growing in the middle of the old convent's courtyard.

She pulled into the section on the right designated for visitor parking and turned off the motor.

More signs on the door of a modern-looking building indicated the business office. It had been attached to the side of the convent, which she imagined was used these days to store the wine.

Rachel touched up her mouth with a coral frost lipstick, then alighted from the car with her briefcase.

It was a good thing she'd learned long ago to wear comfortable leather sandals while on business. Negotiating the cobblestones with some semblance of dignity was no small feat.

On her way inside she counted a dozen cars. That meant a busy Monday for the staff who'd opened their wine cellar to customers eager to sample everything from Riesling to Pinot Blanc.

Rachel imagined the tourist traffic was non-stop, even in the low season.

Once she stepped inside, the receptionist in the foyer looked up from the computer and smiled. *"Bonjour, mademoiselle."*

"Bonjour, madame," Rachel responded in kind.

But her accent must have given her away because the other woman said in excellent English, "The *cave* is through that door on your right."

"Thank you. However I've come on business, and would like to meet with the owner." She handed the other woman her business card.

"My name is Rachel Valentine. I'm the chief wine buyer for three restaurants in London, each called the Bella Lucia."

The receptionist eyed her with renewed interest. "Valentine, you say? I can't find your name on the computer. Was Monsieur Chartier expecting you?"

"No. In fact I didn't know of the Domaine Chartier until I arrived in Thann early today."

"I see."

"When I asked the hotel concierge to direct me to the best vineyard in the region, he gave me directions to the convent."

"Monsieur Chartier will be happy to hear it."

"Naturally I realize he might be too busy to meet with me today, so I'd like to make an appointment for tomorrow if that's possible."

"We're closed tomorrow, but let me check with his secretary and find out his schedule. He has other vineyards in different villages, so he could be anywhere. Excuse me for a moment, please."

"Of course."

Rachel had studied enough French to speak and understand basic phrases, but the receptionist's volley of French spoken in a low rapid tone was much too fast for her to follow.

After the woman hung up she said, "If you'll let me know where you can be reached, Monsieur Chartier's secretary will give him the information."

"That would be fine. I'm staying at the Hotel du Roi."

"Très bien. Though I can't give you an exact time, you'll be contacted before the end of the day."

"Thank you for your help."

"Pas de quoi, mademoiselle."

Rachel went out to the car and returned to the hotel where she caught up on some paperwork.

Around five-thirty her stomach made noises it was time to eat. She decided to try the hotel's restaurant.

In case someone tried to reach her at the hotel rather than on her cell, she told the concierge she'd be in the dining room if a call from Domaine Chartier came through for her.

Whenever Rachel traveled, she always found it instructive to study the wine list and find out what local wines were served, especially in an area like this renowned for its white varietals—wine that came from one kind of grape only.

She wasn't surprised Domaine Chartier wines dominated the choices. The *serveuse* recommended the Tokay Pinot Gris to accompany the asparagus entrée, the hotel's *plat du jour.*

The moment the waitress returned with the wine, Rachel thanked her, examined the labeling and then opened the bottle herself. An aroma escaped from the golden liquid whose combination of flavors was pure revelation.

She poured some into the wineglass and took an experimental sip, letting it swirl on her tongue before swallowing.

More flavors came through: maple syrup, quince and…pineapple if she wasn't mistaken.

So soft to the palate, yet beautifully rich and elegant due to its fine ripe acid balance…

It had a long finish in which she could find no fault.

Ah…perfection itself.

"I take it the Pinot Gris pleases you." A deep male voice spoke to her in English with a heavy French accent.

Her eyelids fluttered open in surprise. But when she saw who it was, she nearly fell off her chair.

"You!"

Across the small round table from her stood the man who'd come close to crashing into her earlier.

For a Frenchman he was tall and powerfully built. Probably in his mid-thirties. He wore his dark brown hair considerably longer than most men she knew.

With his heavily lashed brown eyes and olive complexion, she had to admit he was incredibly handsome.

That, plus the fact that he had the audacity to be holding her wine bottle in his hand, ignited her anger all over again.

"If you've followed me for any other reason than to offer sincere apologies for your reckless driving, I'll call the police to have you arrested for harassment."

The maddening smile she remembered flashed once more.

"There are two versions to every story. The police are more likely to believe that you were all over the road because you're used to driving on the left and became confused."

"Considering they're French, they probably will," she countered. "Now that you've had your fun, please leave that wine bottle on the table and go away."

"I noticed you enjoying it."

He wasn't about to quit.

No doubt this man, who was too attractive by far and knew it, found it amusing to flirt with what he considered an available female. Particularly one drinking alone in public and enjoying it so much she'd been sitting there with her head tilted back, eyes closed, unaware of the people around her.

"Not that it's any of your business, but it happens to be the best white wine I've ever tasted." And that was saying a lot...

He seemed to ponder her comment before he said, "I'm glad to hear it, Ms Valentine. Nineteen ninety-eight produced an excellent vintage."

She blinked. "How do you know my name? Who are you?"

He put the bottle back on the table. "Luc Chartier. I understand you wanted to make an appointment with me."

He was *that* Chartier?

Rachel sat up straighter in the chair. "I thought your secretary was going to phone. I had no idea you would take the trouble to come to the hotel this evening."

He gave an elegant shrug of his broad shoulders covered in a light gray silk suit. "Why not? I was in the area when I received a call from my secretary, Philippe.

"It's always a pleasure to meet a new wine buyer, especially one who has already sampled the goods with such uninhibited relish."

His lips twitched again, rekindling her anger.

"Because of you, I almost missed the experience."

He cocked his dark head. "What do you say we call a truce to the Hundred Years War and start over again? You've already admitted the Pinot Gris has no equal. I'd like to make up for the fright I caused you by giving you a personal tour of the *domaine*."

Rachel rolled her eyes. "In that rocket you call a car? No, thank you. I have little desire to end up as twisted wreckage around a bunch of grape vines."

"I'll make a concession and drive you in the estate Wagoneer," he inserted. "That way we can go off road. I swear I've never had an accident with any of my prospective buyers."

She believed him. Yet even if it weren't true, Rachel imagined his charisma got him what he wanted no matter how audacious he was. But not this time.

"I'm afraid I've changed my mind about making an appointment."

"I prefer to be spontaneous too," he came back. "What are your plans after dinner?"

"Surely that's not any of your business."

He examined the shape of her oval face until her cheeks grew warm.

"The last thing I meant to do was frighten you on the road today. I'll admit I had serious matters on my mind. Forgive me."

Forgive him?

Where had that apology come from? It sounded a hundred percent genuine.

She could feel the ice cracking.

"Whether you do any business with me or not, I'd like to make it up to you, Ms Valentine.

"If you'll give me half an hour, I'll come back for you. While we talk wine, we'll take a ride through the vineyard. Now that it's in flower, it's especially beautiful at dusk."

Rachel sat back. "You're making this very difficult for me. If I refuse to accept your apology, then I come off being the lesser person." After a slight hesitation, "I suppose it's possible I was so enthralled with the view, I forgot I wasn't the only driver on the road."

"An honest woman," he murmured.

"A man who can say he's sorry. I guess we're even."

"*Pax?*"

Rachel nodded. "*Pax.* I'd be a liar if I didn't admit I'd enjoy seeing your vineyard. But only if you're sure it's all right with your wife."

There was a distinct pause before he said, "If I weren't divorced, my wife would be the one showing you around. As it is, you're stuck with me."

"Since you're the owner of Chartier et Fils, I have no complaints," she quipped to hide a myriad feelings she didn't dare examine too closely.

Some unnamed emotion produced a glimmer in the dark recesses of his eyes. It caused her pulse to race for no good reason.

"In that case, I suggest you change into something casual. Lovely as your outfit is, you won't find it suitable if you want to get out and do a little walking."

"I'm sure you're right."

"Until you're surrounded by the vines, you can't fully appreciate what a miracle they are."

He'd just expressed the thoughts she'd always held.

Whatever else went on inside him, she sensed he was a man who was in love with his work. Apology aside, not many vintners she'd met cared enough to go out of their way to this extent for a buyer.

"What color is your Wagoneer?

"Blue."

"I'll watch for you."

"*Bon.* Enjoy the rest of your meal. *A bientôt.*"

As he walked away Rachel noticed that quite a few interested female eyes followed his progress from the room.

After eating a little more of the delicious vegetable entrée, she charged the bill to her room, then went upstairs to change. She took the wine bottle with her for a souvenir of her first day in Alsace.

Once she'd slipped into jeans and a plum-colored knit top, she put on a pair of well-used walking shoes she'd packed in her suitcase.

With twenty more minutes to wait until he returned, she decided to do something productive in order not to think too much.

Before she'd agreed to go with him, she'd been so furious, she'd actually shouted names at him. That was something she'd never done to anyone in her life.

Not wanting to think about how badly she'd lost control, or, worse, how easily he'd won her around, she decided now would be a good time to make a call to the UK.

Pulling out her cell phone, she punched in the digits. After three rings a familiar male voice answered.

"Grandfather? It's Rachel."

"How's my Black Beauty this even—"

But before he could even finish the question, a coughing spell ensued. The doctor explained it was to be expected with a pulmonary embolism, yet it still alarmed her.

"Just a minute," he said in a croaky voice.

"Take all the time you need."

She adored her Grandfather William, who'd called her his Black Beauty from the time she was a little girl.

Though she'd grown up tall and slender, her thick hair had some brown mixed in with the black, but he didn't worry about small technicalities.

He'd given her the book of the same name before her mother had taken her and Rebecca to live in New York when they were ten.

His present for Rebecca had been a magnificently illustrated book of *Sleeping Beauty*.

"These are so that neither of my little beauties will forget me," he'd whispered in a loving voice.

"I don't want to leave you and Daddy," Rachel cried between sobs. The divorce between his son Robert and their American mother, Diana, had taken a traumatic toll on the entire family.

His gray eyes moistened. "I know. Sometimes we have to do

things we don't like to do. But I'll come to visit you, and when you and Rebecca fly to London to stay with your father, you'll have sleepovers with your grandmother and me."

True to his word, there were sleepovers, and her grandparents did make trips back and forth from the UK to Long Island when they could get away from the restaurant business long enough.

On those occasions he would say, "You're the thoroughbred of the Valentine family, Rachel. Of course, you inherited your mother's famous Crawford smile and her large blue eyes. On you their tinge of gray gives them a wistful quality.

"Now that you're becoming such a lovely woman, you're going to have to protect yourself from the many men who will want a relationship with you."

Rachel had taken everything her beloved grandfather had told her so much to heart, she'd reached the ripe old age of thirty-three and was still single.

Over the course of the years she'd met a lot of appealing men in her position as wine buyer for her grandfather's restaurants. However none of them was the right kind of man to marry because none of them measured up to him. Not in character or kindness.

But a little while ago something of significance had transpired, though surely not the *coup de foudre* her grandfather had always warned her about.

"Love at first sight. When I was in Italy during the Second World War, that's what Lucia and I experienced. Fortunately for me, she was the right kind of woman to marry.

"Your grandmother and I were completely happy together. I want that same happiness for you when you meet your beloved. You'll know when it happens."

Rachel scoffed at the romantic notion that such a thing could happen.

Still, she couldn't ignore certain emotions Monsieur Chartier had evoked. When she'd opened her eyes and had seen *him* standing there eyeing her so…intimately, she'd felt an explosion inside her that had never happened to her before.

"Rachel? Are you still there?"

Her grandfather seemed to have recovered from his coughing episode.

"Where else would I be? I want to know what Dr Lloyd had to say today."

"To quote him, I'm 'coming along'."

"That's wonderful news. Now I can enjoy my business trip without worrying too much."

"What I'd have given to come with you."

"We'll do it when you're all better. But since you have to rest right now, I'll think of something to make up for it.

"I'd bring you home a bottle of your favorite Châteauneuf du Pape, but with those blood clots in your lungs, I know alcohol is *verboten*, so I'll bring you a box of chocolate truffles instead."

"Always my thoughtful girl. How much longer will you be gone?"

"A week."

Because of this detour to Thann she needed two. But considering he'd been in and out of hospital several times for pain and shortness of breath, she would have to take this a day at a time.

"Did you say hello to Vincent for me when you visited the Rolland vineyards in St Emilion?"

"Of course. He sent his regards and has extended you an invitation to visit as soon as you're better."

"That's nice."

"His father also told me to say hello to you. He's looking forward to another game of chess with you the next time you come."

"He likes to win."

Rachel chuckled. "I'm afraid chess isn't my best suit either."

"Where are yo—?" But before he could finish, another bout of coughing had started up.

"In Thann." Anticipating his next question, she said, "I haven't located Louis Delacroix yet, but I will. Right now you need to stop talking and drink some water. I'm going to say goodnight. I'll call you tomorrow evening."

"Bl-bless you, Rachel. GoodNIGHT." The second part came out with another loud cough.

Supposedly the coughing meant he was getting rid of the dead cells off his lungs, which was a good thing.

She hung up, put the phone back in her purse and hurried down the hall, nodding to some of the guests coming up the stairs.

When she emerged from the lobby doors, she discovered Monsieur Chartier lounging against the body of the Wagoneer parked directly in front.

The sight of him pushed the worry over her grandfather to the back of her mind.

He'd changed into a soft yellow sport shirt and blue jeans that hugged his long, rock-hard legs.

She lost the battle not to stare at the strong column of his throat and the smattering of dark body hair.

Their eyes met for a stunning moment. Though she might be a mature businesswoman, this striking man had the power to reduce her to a moonstruck teen without doing one thing to entice her—except to exist.

But, as Rachel had just found out, existence was more than enough to keep her from concentrating with any degree of coherence.

The moment he saw her, he unfolded his suntanned arms and opened the passenger door for her.

As she moved past him to climb inside she felt a disturbing awareness of him she didn't want to feel because he was a new business acquaintance. He wasn't supposed to mean anything more to her.

If being in his presence was going to cause her to forget why she'd come to Thann, she'd better start interacting with him on a professional basis.

Once they'd left the town she said, "I drove past your vineyard on the way to the convent. It looked a lot larger than the ones I passed on my drive from Colmar."

"You're very observant. There are less than six thousand vineyards in Alsace. Of that amount four thousand of them are only five acres or less each."

"So small?"

He nodded. "After Alsace fell back into French hands from the Germans, we had to build up our wine industry all over again.

"My grandfather went from village to village, buying up a few acres here, a few there.

"Today we have a total of five hundred acres located in seven villages. This vineyard of three hundred acres is an exception."

"That means a lot of little babies to nurture."

He turned his dark head toward her.

"Babies?" The way his native tongue caused him to pronounce the English word charmed her in ways she couldn't describe.

"Yes. Fragile under certain circumstances, strong under others. Always needing love and care."

"An interesting analogy, one I'll have to pass on to my staff."

He sounded genuinely amused, as if his thoughts had been far away, yet somehow her comment had managed to penetrate his consciousness.

When they reached the convent, he kept on going. In a few minutes he made a left onto a dirt road that bisected part of the vineyard.

Twilight had descended over Thann. She lowered the window. A gentle breeze filled the interior with warm air still rising from the sun-soaked soil.

He brought their vehicle to a stop and turned off the motor.

"We'll go on foot from here. Maybe if we listen closely, we'll hear growing pains."

Rachel let out a gentle laugh before climbing down without his help. She didn't want to risk an accidental touch. Already her thoughts about him had grown out of proportion to the occasion.

She followed his lead as they worked their way down two rows of vines in flower on either side of them.

Like her father and grandfather, he was tall, yet he moved with a certain masculine litheness. In fact he seemed part of this fusion of man to nature, as if neither could be separated from the other.

While she reflected on how in tune he was with his ancestral roots, he stopped long enough to scoop up a handful of earth.

Turning to her, he held out his hand.

"Like the seed a man plants in a woman's womb that brings

life from God, so the seed of the Riesling grape lies cocooned in this particular blend of soil found nowhere else on earth."

The analogy shook her to the core.

"What are the components?"

"You really want to know?" His question was straightforward, yet tinged with a hint of mockery.

She couldn't blame him if he thought she was a typical female buyer whose attraction to him was strong enough that she would say or do anything to prolong their time together.

Rachel *was* guilty of having feelings that had nothing to do with grapes or wine-making. In truth, now that she'd gotten over being angry, she found herself intrigued by him, not just his life's work.

"I wouldn't have asked otherwise," she came back, striving for a steady voice. "The more I learn, the more I find out I don't know, but I *want* to learn as much as I can."

"Then you're a rare species."

She held his enigmatic gaze. "Since I'm fortunate enough to be in the presence of a master vintner, I realize my good fortune. So let me warn you that I'm prepared to pick your brains for as long as you're willing to indulge me."

The second those words came out of her mouth, she couldn't believe she'd said them. He probably thought she was flirting with him. Maybe subconsciously she was. What on earth was wrong with her?

In the fading light she couldn't see the expression in his eyes, but she felt them studying her intently before he answered her question.

"Limestone, granite, clay, marl—"

"Marl?"

"A crumbly mixture of clays, carbonates, shells and magnesium. Each vineyard's soil is different and suitable for a certain kind of grape.

"Did you know, for instance, that wild grape vines grew here before the Romans domesticated them?"

"How fascinating! Even then the conditions were perfect," she said in awe.

"Yes. The aroma you enjoyed from the Tokay grape earlier this evening came from the soil at St Hippolyte."

"It was wonderful!" she exclaimed. "I detected woodsmoke, a touch of honey and something else I still can't identify."

"Licorice?"

"Yes!" she cried softly.

His eyes gleamed. "I have to admit I'm impressed, *mademoiselle*."

Evidently she'd passed some sort of initial test or he wouldn't have said anything.

He shifted his weight. It threw his profile into relief, drawing her attention to the lines bracketing his mouth.

Whatever his experiences of life, which included the grief of divorce, they lent him a brooding demeanor. Yet his sensual appeal was so compelling, she had to tear her eyes away.

"It would take more than a lifetime to learn everything you know, *monsieur*, so don't mind me if I hang on to every word."

His eyes smiled. "In that case I'll tell you the most important thing to remember. You won't ever detect that same aroma again if it comes from a different *terroir*."

A wry smile broke out on her face. "I'm going to hold you to that claim and sample every type of wine from your various vineyards."

After a slight pause, "That could take some time."

"How many wines do you produce?"

"Sixteen."

A higher figure than she'd presumed. He'd just provided her with an excuse to linger in his kingdom a little longer. But if she were wise, she wouldn't give in to that temptation or he would know she'd lost sight of her professional objective because of her growing attraction to him.

"Now I'm the one impressed," she declared. "What days are your wine cellars open? I know tomorrow you're closed."

He let the soil fall from his hand. "Nevertheless I'll ask my manager, Giles Lambert, to phone you and make himself available in the morning.

"The old man's a walking encyclopedia of information. He'll

be delighted to brainwash you into making Domaine Chartier your exclusive white wine source."

With those words, Monsieur Chartier had just brought this unexpected interlude to a close. Knowing he wouldn't be around tomorrow should have eased her mind, yet she felt a strong sense of disappointment, which was ridiculous.

Hopefully her expression didn't give her away. "If it won't be an imposition for him."

"He lives to talk about our precious vines."

Her mouth curved upward. "Then I assure you I'll be a captive audience. The Tokay I was served at dinner convinced me I don't need to look elsewhere this trip.

"One thing I've learned about wine—I don't like being overwhelmed by too many choices. I'd rather concentrate on your Pinot Gris and Riesling while I'm here."

"You're very wise," he muttered, sounding as if her comment had surprised him. "If you're ready, I'll take you back to the hotel."

Unable to help it, she found herself examining his firm jaw and the slight cleft in his chin. Her gaze wandered higher to his straight nose. He had well-shaped brows. All in all the arrangement in such a patently masculine face made him irresistible.

Rachel didn't want to leave the vineyard yet, but he'd given her no choice. He had some place else to go.

Walking ahead of him, she reached the Wagoneer first and got inside before he could assist her.

He didn't seem inclined to talk. When she thought about it, she realized he hadn't asked her one personal question. There'd been no show of curiosity on his part, not even about the kind of restaurants she represented.

Rachel on the other hand was the one guilty of so many unanswered personal questions about him, she was ready to burst.

Yet she realized that a man like him didn't come along often. To imagine he might be available to her, let alone interested, was absurd.

Any woman who misread the signals and tried to step over the invisible line he'd drawn would soon feel the fool.

What she should do was thank him for deputizing his venerable vineyard manager to educate her about the fabulous wines the Chartier family had produced for generations.

But she refrained from saying anything when she sensed a curious tension coming from him since they'd driven away from the vineyard.

As he maneuvered the curve that led them back to town she noticed the way his suntanned fingers tightened almost compulsively on the steering wheel.

Evidently he had something serious on his mind far removed from the possible sale of wine to some nebulous restaurants in the UK.

Was it the same thing that had been on his mind earlier today right before their near miss?

Not wanting him to think she expected tonight's experience to be repeated, the second he pulled up in front of the hotel she opened the door and slid out while the motor was still running.

Facing him the way she would any business person at the end of a successful meeting, she said, "You've made my introduction to Alsatian wines the highlight of my trip."

"Even if our initial meeting caused you some tense moments?"

She smiled. "Even then. Seriously, I'd like to thank you for giving me this much time. I'm looking forward to meeting with your manager tomorrow. Goodbye, *monsieur.*"

She shut the door.

If he said anything in response, she didn't hear it as she hurried inside the hotel.

Since she wouldn't be seeing him again, she intended to put all personal thoughts of him out of her mind.

After reaching her room, she picked up the bottle of Tokay and opened it once more to inhale the aroma.

Licorice… Of course. He knew all its secrets.

Too exhilarated to think of sleeping yet, she set up her laptop and began recording the evening's events.

She didn't want to leave out a single piece of information or a bit of wisdom he'd imparted. One day all this research would go into her book.

When she finally went to bed, she was still reliving the time spent with him.

"Please don't let *him* be too unforgettable," she begged of the darkness before closing her eyes.

CHAPTER TWO

ON THE forty-minute drive back to St Hippolyte, Lucien Chartier, whom everyone called Luc, got on his cell phone to Giles.

"We have a potential buyer from the UK staying in Thann at the Hotel du Roi. According to Philippe, Mademoiselle Valentine buys for three London restaurants, all called the Bella Lucia.

"I asked him to check them out for me. They've been established since nineteen forty-six and are reputed to be some of the most exclusive restaurants located in London."

Mayfair, Chelsea and Knightsbridge wouldn't mean anything to Giles, but Luc knew exactly what kind of upscale, international clientele visited such establishments.

Many famous actors and musicians from the swinging sixties had made the original restaurant famous. Between all three restaurants, three hundred and fifty people were served on a nightly basis.

Nothing could please Luc more than to know that Domaine Chartier would be gracing the tables at Bella Lucia in future. Little by little the world was getting acquainted with Alsatian white wines.

"Do me a favor and give her the royal treatment tomorrow. She's surprisingly intuitive about wine. What she doesn't know, she's eager to learn. That's where you come in, Giles."

The older man made a sound in his throat. "I haven't met many women buyers from the UK."

"Nor have I."

In fact she didn't have a strong British accent. There'd been moments when he could have sworn she was American. Rachel Valentine was a surprise in more ways than one.

For one thing, he hadn't thought she would forgive him. To his surprise she was willing to admit some culpability. An unusual woman.

Once they'd gotten past that hurdle, she'd shown an uncommon interest in the whole business of wine culture. There was a great deal more to her than the surface revealed.

An exceptionally beautiful surface, standing there in the vines.

The gentle night breeze had swirled her hair into a cloud of brunette silk. He'd watched it swirl around other parts of her as well, molding the top she was wearing to her lovely body.

He tried to force his thoughts to stop right there, but they filled his mind anyway.

Since first passing her on the road, then seeing her in the hotel dining room enjoying herself to the fullest, it shocked him to discover he was having difficulty controlling certain pictures of the two of them that wouldn't leave him alone. Breathtaking pictures he shouldn't be entertaining. Not with Paulette lying comatose in her hospital bed.

Guilt over his ex-wife's condition caused him to drive faster, but the image of Ms Valentine tasting the wine seemed to be emblazoned in his psyche.

At first he'd thought she'd imbibed too much wine like so many other buyers anxious to sample everything at once.

Taking advantage of the moment had given him time to study her feminine profile—the way the white material of her expensive suit followed the lines and curves of her slender figure.

He'd felt a quickening in his body that hadn't happened for so long, he couldn't remember the last time. Years…

Troubled by the involuntary reaction over which he'd had no control, he'd plucked the bottle from the table, curious to know how much she'd consumed.

When he'd realized it was still full, his glance had flown to her wineglass, which had contained only a small residue of wine.

At that point his eyes had fastened helplessly on her pomegranate-red mouth, then her tender throat exposed to his gaze where he'd watched her savoring her first swallow of the velvety liquid.

Mon Dieu. He'd never seen anything so provocative in his life.

His hand tightened on his cell phone. "Since she wants to concentrate on the Tokay and Riesling, I suspect she could be here for a few days. Call me when you've taken her order."

"I'll make certain it's a big one," Giles promised.

"Why do you think I gave you the responsibility?"

Though it was inevitable for Luc to come in contact with attractive women, he was reluctant to be around her again. She'd awakened something inside him totally unexpected.

"If you need to get in touch with me tomorrow, I'll be at the hospital. Just leave a message on my voice mail and I'll get back to you. Otherwise I'll see you at the banquet."

"D'accord."

He hung up, relieved to have put Giles in charge of Ms Valentine. Out of sight, out of mind.

As for tonight, the single best way to cure what was ailing him was to drop by the hospital in St Hippolyte.

Needing to ignore what had happened tonight, he drove straight to the long-term-care medical facility and hurried inside. After three years, it had become his second home.

To his surprise he met Yves Brouet's accusing stare when he walked in Paulette's room a few minutes later. That was all he needed.

She lay in a coma between them. Only the sound of the machines keeping Luc's ex-wife alive made any noise.

Normally the two men staggered their times in order to spread out the visits. And to avoid each other. Luc usually went there in the morning before putting in a full day's work.

"Holy Mother of God, Luc—how long are you going to fight the family on this?"

As he'd just come from battling his attraction to a certain wine buyer from the UK his dark eyes glittered with a mixture of fresh guilt and pain. "For as long as it takes."

"Let my sister go. Let this be finished so she can rest in peace!"

Luc's hands formed fists. He leaned over to kiss the forehead of her thin face before walking out of the room into the hall.

He refused to allow any arguing in front of Paulette. On some level he was convinced she could hear and understand what was going on. It horrified him that Yves had talked about her dying while standing next to her bed.

The other man followed him into the corridor. "My sister's gone. You have no right to prolong this agony."

After being best friends from childhood, it didn't seem possible the two of them had come to this impasse.

"I'm paying for her care, Yves."

"Money be damned. We're talking about Paulette. She wouldn't have wanted this. You *know* she wouldn't!"

"That's easy for us to say since we're not the one in there fighting for life."

Yves' face screwed up in pain. "That's no life. You might as well know now. Since there isn't any reasoning with you, the family got together last month. We've hired an attorney to fight you in court and get these infernal machines turned off."

"I know," Luc whispered. "My attorney already informed me." It was only a matter of time before Luc's sister Giselle found out.

Thank God his new house was ready to move into so he could live on his own again. Between his mother who backed him, and Giselle who sided with Yves and fought him at every opportunity, Luc hadn't had a moment's peace in the last year.

"You can't win, Luc. You're not her husband. The only reason we gave you this long before getting legal counsel is because of our families' longstanding friendship over the years. But because of this insanity of yours, that's gone…disappeared."

That was right. Because of Luc, Paulette had been consigned to a living death. But not if he could help it.

He shifted his weight. "I'm planning on her waking up, Yves. When she does, I'll do whatever I can to help her get on with her life."

Yves plowed fingers through hair as blond as Paulette's. "No, Luc. Your responsibility to her is over. Even if Paulette were to wake up and make a full recovery, she wouldn't want you involved."

Luc closed his eyes tightly for a minute. "*When* she wakes up, I intend to be here for her."

"Could it be you're confusing guilt and remorse with love?"

Those words stung. "I loved your sister. That's why I married her."

"But sometimes love isn't enough. Come on, Luc. That time is long past and now Paulette yearns to escape her body."

If Luc thought that were true…

"This morning *Maman* and *Papa* asked me to talk sense to you one final time. They said that if you really care about her, then prove it and allow her to go free so this madness can end."

Luc shook his dark head. "I can't… All the research I've done on coma patients indicates they respond to their loved ones' stimulation. She could wake up at any time."

Strong hands clasped Luc's cheeks. "But she hasn't, and she won't because she's in a vegetative state. A few sounds and tiny movements over thirty-six months means nothing! So I'm begging you—give it up!" he half sobbed the words before wheeling away.

Luc watched his friend's solid figure until it disappeared around a corner. No one could get to him like Yves, who'd been closer than a brother from childhood.

Overwhelmed by guilt attacking him from every direction, he rested against the wall for a minute and rubbed his eyes with the palms of his hands.

Not only had his four-year marriage ended in failure, Paulette's car accident was his fault.

Talking to Yves had just compounded his guilt because of the pain he'd brought to her family. Besides their grief over her condition, they didn't have the kind of money it took to pay attorney fees.

Had Luc become such a selfish bastard, he didn't care who got hurt any more as long as he got his own way?

Crucified once more by Yves' tortured plea, Luc went back to her bedside to say goodnight.

When he left the hospital, he passed by the nursing station to let them know he was on his way out. They had his cell-phone number and knew to call him day or night if there was any change in her condition.

Luc left the hospital aware there was no change in Paulette. *There would never be a change*.

That was what everyone was telling him, including his sister's husband.

Jean-Marc was a good man, but he and Giselle never missed an opportunity to remind him it was Paulette's family who had the last say in the matter.

Her parents had brought her into the world and raised her. They wanted what they felt was best for their daughter. It was their God-given right after all.

Rights.

How Luc hated that word.

Yves had spoken the truth when he'd said Luc had no legal grounds to fight their family.

But wanting Paulette to wake up from that coma didn't have anything to do with rights.

At the core of his anguish lay the need to rid his soul of a burden growing increasingly heavy.

He'd had three years to come to terms with the divorce. What haunted him was the inability to go back to the day of her accident and prevent it.

Ever since he'd found out she was lying unconscious in the hospital, he hadn't ceased begging her forgiveness. But he didn't know if she'd heard him.

Once her family made the decision to turn off the machines, there wouldn't be a possibility of her hearing him, let alone forgiving him.

He hit his fist against his palm.

Once again it all got down to what *he* wanted, as if the universe revolved around him.

One word from him to the Brouet family and everything would change for them.

On the surface he had to admit life would change for him, too. No more daily trips to the hospital.

But inwardly nothing else would be different. Remorse over the accident that didn't need to have happened stifled life's possibilities.

Once back in his Wagoneer, his pain and frustration were further aggravated by the faint smell of roses that still lingered in the car's interior. Sensitive to fragrances all his life, he was haunted by Ms Valentine's scent.

It appeared this visit to the hospital hadn't rooted her out of his system the way he could prune a vine and make a clean cut of the unwanted cane.

Part of him resented her intrusion at this critical period in his life. Just the thought of her opened the floodgates to his private thoughts.

Once again he was bombarded by unbidden pictures he hadn't been able to expel from his consciousness.

He revved up the engine, and his tires squealed as he left the parking lot. In a few minutes he reached his mother's home where he'd been living temporarily. But he was so conflicted by feelings and emotions tearing him apart, he knew there'd be no sleep for him tonight.

Because of a certain enigmatic Frenchman, Rachel tossed and turned during the long, dark hours of the night. Relieved when the light of dawn crept into the room, she showered and got dressed in a silky cream blouse and tan skirt for her work day with Giles Lambert.

He'd phoned her last night to make the arrangements, promising her a thorough tour of the winery.

Like her grandfather, he had a zest for life and possessed so much charm she was already predisposed to like him.

She could only hope a productive day spent with him would take away her disappointment that it wasn't Luc Chartier doing the honors. Part of her feared that, when she left Alsace, no ploy would be able to banish him from her thoughts.

Like a comet that only passed near the earth once in a lifetime, he'd left his indelible impression on her, then hurtled on into deep space supposedly out of mind and sight.

Maybe when her grandfather had recovered from his latest bout of illness, the two of them could come back to Alsace so she could legitimately meet with the owner of the Chartier vineyards again.

Legitimately…

Good heavens—she was as bad as a teenager plotting ways to get the most gorgeous guy in the world to be interested in her. It seemed her attraction to him was so intense, she wasn't above using her grandfather to accomplish her objective.

Filled with self-disgust, Rachel grabbed her cell phone to put in her purse before going downstairs to eat breakfast. To her surprise it rang before she could leave the room.

For one foolish moment she thought it might be the man whose image had haunted her all night. Just the thought of hearing his deep voice caused her heart to leap. She clicked on eagerly, not bothering to check the caller ID.

"H-hello?" she answered, sounding out of breath, because she was!

"Rachel—"

Her spirits dropped like hot rocks.

"Dad—

"Something must be wrong for you to be calling me this early in the morning."

Normally he didn't show up at work until ten-thirty or later. But evidently a problem had arisen and he needed someone to bark at, mainly her.

He always sounded impatient when he was at the restaurant he managed with her half brother Max. Since every day was hectic behind the scenes, she supposed he could be forgiven.

But being this far away and hearing him so abrupt with her caught her off guard.

"What's this I hear about you traveling to Alsace? I don't recall us discussing a stop there. Today's the fifteenth. Your itinerary says you're supposed to be in Champagne."

Uh oh. Somehow her grandfather must have let it slip. Not that it was a secret.

Clearing her throat, she said, "Grandfather asked me to look up an old friend in Thann as a special favor."

"So I've heard, but I don't want you spending too much time there. We can't afford to slight our other suppliers."

Her temperamental father knew her better than that, but he had to say it because she hadn't obtained his seal of approval first.

"I wouldn't do that, and I've already contacted Monsieur Bulot to let him know I'll be there in a few days.

"The point is, now that I'm here I'm doing a little research, so please don't worry."

"You've been to Angers, then?"

"Of course, and St Emilion. They're filling our orders as we speak, so you needn't be concerned."

Her explanation appeared to mollify him somewhat because his curiosity finally won out enough to ask, "Have you come across anything interesting?"

Rachel's eyes closed tightly.

It wouldn't be possible to answer his question with one succinct answer. Too much had happened since she'd met Luc Chartier. Getting to know him had done something to her. But it was too soon to find the right words to describe what was going on inside her.

"I'm discovering that Alsace is a land of enchantment. I'll tell you all about it when I get home." She needed to change the subject. "How is Grandfather? What about his pulse-ox level?"

"I never got the chance to find out. Last night John barged in, so I left."

The rivalry between her dad and his half brother reminded her of her own unwitting problems with her sister. They lived too far apart with Rebecca working in New York as a highly successful advertising executive.

Though they were unidentical and conducted different lives, they were alike in dozens of small ways. Rachel knew instinctively Rebecca would be enamoured of Alsace too. How sad they couldn't have shared a trip like this.

She heaved a troubled sigh. This morning she didn't want to think about insoluble family problems.

"Dad? I have to go, but I'll call you when I get to Champagne."

"Don't stay in Alsace too long."

"I won't." She frowned. "What else is bothering you? You sound more upset than usual this morning."

"Titan stepped on a rusty nail. The vet took care of him, but he's not himself yet."

Translated, the Dobermann had been well sedated. Too bad that couldn't be his permanent condition.

"I'm sure he'll be back to normal in no time."

Her father's dog made everyone nervous, even Rachel. She preferred Saffy, the miniature poodle who belonged to her father's wife, Bev. The poor little thing cowered every time she saw Titan coming.

That was exactly what Rachel did when her father felt threatened by John and became difficult, which was most of the time these days.

"I'll talk to you soon, Dad."

She hung up the phone, thankful to have found a small corner of paradise here in Thann where she could put that seething cauldron of tension aside for a little while.

A few minutes later she entered the hotel dining room. During those times when she had to sample wines, she always ate a good meal first, even if she wasn't hungry. Today was a case in point. Luc Chartier's stranglehold on her feelings seemed to have affected her appetite as well.

Luc couldn't swallow the croissant, let alone his coffee. He pushed himself away from the breakfast table and got to his feet, startling his mother.

"Where are you going at this early hour?"

"To the hospital. Where else?"

"But you were there late last night—has something happened to Paulette you haven't told us about?"

"*Maman—*" Giselle blurted impatiently. "Surely if there'd been any change in her condition, we would all know about it."

She switched her dark gaze to Luc, "But I have to admit I'm curious why all this extra vigilance over her. What's going on with you, *mon frère?*"

That was a question he couldn't answer yet.

"I've been so busy lately, I decided to spend quality time with her. Dr Soulier says the more stimulation, the better."

"As you should do," his mother remarked.

Giselle threw her napkin down. "Why do you encourage him, *Maman?* After three years, we all know she's not going to wake up."

"None of us knows that," Luc countered. "As long as there's a chance, I'm going to do everything in my power to make it happen."

"I don't understand this obsession," Giselle cried in frustration.

"I *do*," their mother snapped. "Despite a piece of paper, Luc is still married to her in the eyes of God, and don't you forget it, *ma fille!*"

At this point Giselle was on her feet. Her eyes looked suspiciously bright as she turned to him. "I can't stand to see you go on like this."

He and Giselle had always been close, but the situation with Paulette had strained their relationship.

"After today you and Jean-Marc won't have to. I'm sleeping at my new house from now on, starting tonight."

"So soon?" his mother questioned. "I was hoping you would stay here a little longer. Since your *papa* died, I love having my children around."

He kissed her cheek. "We all need our space, *Maman.*"

"But you have no one to cook for you."

"That's the least of my worries."

"Well, it's one of mine! I'll be by to bring you some food so you won't starve to death."

Giselle eyed him soulfully. "Paulette's not going to wake up. You do know that, don't you?"

"Enough!" their mother cried, pointing her finger at Giselle. "You have your hands full taking care of your own husband and children. I would like to see how you would react if it were Jean-Marc lying in that hospital bed."

Giselle's cheeks went a ruddy color. "If we were already divorced, I can assure you I wouldn't have stayed at his bedside three years waiting for the impossible to happen."

"Nothing's impossible," their mother said firmly.

Giselle continued to look at Luc. "Remember what *Papa* always said? There comes a time when we must *laissez-le de se faire.*"

Trust his vintner sister to remind him of the old expression their father lived by.

Don't add anything artificial to the process. Leave the wine to do what it is meant to do.

Translated, let Paulette's family decide to shut off the machines and then see what happens.

Tears filled her eyes. "You're not meant to live a monk's life. At this rate you're going to have a breakdown."

Breakdown.

An interesting choice of words his guilt hadn't allowed him to contemplate since last evening, when he'd first laid eyes on Rachel Valentine. A woman like her didn't need a man with his kind of baggage.

"I have to go."

"That's all you have to say?"

Giselle was in pain for him, but right now he was too fragmented by opposing forces to think. At this point it felt as if all his energy was focused on the beautiful wine buyer from the UK who was less than an hour away from here.

"Tell the children I'll be over soon to take them to the park."

Luc pressed a kiss to her cheek, and another one to his mother's. Then he strode out of the house to his car and drove away. But when he reached the crossroads where he would normally turn left into town, he yanked the wheel to the right and took off for Thann as if unseen hands were driving the car for him.

Rachel pulled into the courtyard of the convent. There were no other cars in the parking area. She was being given exclusive treatment by Luc Chartier's right hand and ought to be thrilled about it.

A trim man with thinning brown hair came out the door to greet her. He looked to be about her grandfather's age, but, unlike him, this man was in excellent health.

When she commented that he moved like a person twenty years younger, he said, "Blame it on the fruit of the vine."

Rachel knew better. Giles had been blessed with good genes. So had her grandfather. But two years ago he'd gone into the hospital with blood clots in his legs, and had been bothered by them on and off ever since.

"I feel guilty that you're spending your day off to show me around, Monsieur Lambert."

"Call me Giles. There's no reason to feel guilty. With my wife gone, I need to keep busy. This is a pleasure for me, and Luc knows it. Come along and we'll get started."

"Thank you."

She followed him inside and through the door to the *cave*.

It was a marvelous room with a vaulted ceiling. There was a long bar and a fabulous stock of wines behind it she was dying to inspect. But what caught her interest was the huge, ancient-looking *armoire* on the wall opposite the counter. The doors remained open to display wine-making artifacts placed behind glass.

Next to it hung a massive chart that walked the layman through an understandable explanation of wine-making. The text was in French, English, German and Spanish.

"This is absolutely fascinating," Rachel declared. "I've never seen anything like it on any of my buying trips."

While she snapped pictures, Giles busied himself putting wine bottles on the counter for her to sample.

"It was Luc's idea so it would cut down on the time the staff spends explaining everything to our customers. As a result, we can handle more clients at a time."

"Genius innovation."

She read everything, then moved in front of the armoire where the items were labeled.

"What a wonderful treasure!"

She took more pictures, but her gaze lingered on an old jade-green flagon. The placard read, "The Chartier family nuptial wine jug. Fourteenth Century."

A cry of delight escaped her throat. "Tell me about this!"

"Which item are you referring to?"

Suddenly the blood pounded in her ears because it wasn't Giles who'd asked the question.

She would know Luc Chartier's heavily accented voice anywhere.

She spun around trying to catch her breath because he'd entered the room without her being aware of it.

"G-good morning," she stammered, attempting to gather her wits. "I thought this was your day off."

He looked fantastic in a gray turtleneck and white cargo pants.

She couldn't prevent her eyes from traveling over his hard, fit body before their gazes fused.

"I decided the things I needed to do today could wait."

His words sent curling warmth through her body.

"What about Giles?"

"He likes to potter around here."

The old man winked at her.

"To borrow your metaphor," Luc said in a low aside, "he's like a mother with a new baby. His work is never done."

"I heard that," Giles muttered. Rachel couldn't help smiling.

Luc studied her as if he enjoyed looking at what he saw. "Now tell me which item in the cupboard fascinates you so much."

As he moved closer she could smell the soap he'd used in the shower. Her senses seemed to have come alive around him.

She turned toward the glass. "The nuptial jug. I'd love to hear the story behind it."

He stood near enough that she could feel his warmth in the cool room whose walls were several feet thick.

"When a Chartier man has found his heart's desire, he pours his favorite wine in that special jug from which he and his beloved both drink, whereupon he declares his undying devotion.

"It's called the marriage ritual of the vine. My father, like his forebears, proposed to my mother in the time-honored Chartier way. They both drank from this jug before they were married in the convent chapel."

Rachel trembled at the evocative image his words had conjured.

She'd been a lover of fairy tales all her life. What he'd just told her was a real-life fairy tale.

How would it be to marry a man like Luc and share in such a thrilling ritual?

He'd told her he was divorced. She couldn't comprehend the pain his ex-wife must feel to live apart from him now.

She cleared her throat. "That's a beautiful story, *monsieur*. Thank you for sharing it with me."

She heard a sharp intake of breath. "After spending time with you last evening, I'm convinced you're one person who can appreciate it."

"Such a ritual is a very romantic tradition."

"You value tradition?" he questioned silkily.

Her gaze flew to his. She swallowed hard to discover his dark brown eyes searching hers.

"Let's just say I envy those who have established traditions to follow. I believe their lives are enriched for them."

He continued to examine her features in the shadowy light, sending ripples of sensual pleasure through her system. How could that be when he wasn't even touching her?

"So do I," his voice rasped. "Now tell me what brought you to Thann besides wine buying."

She blinked. "How did you know there was another reason?"

"Since you hadn't heard of Chartier et Fils until the concierge told you, I assumed you'd ventured into my territory because something else brought you here.

"Be honest. How many people do you know who have ever heard of Thann, let alone could point it out on a map of France?"

His mouth curved upwards, causing her heart to turn over. She couldn't help reciprocating with another smile.

"Actually I do know one person."

When she didn't reveal anything else, his eyes narrowed.

"But you're not going to tell me who it is because it's none of my business. Is that what you're saying?"

"No—" she protested, embarrassed that Giles could hear them. "Not at all—I just don't want to bore you with the details of my personal life when you're such a busy man and have a thriving company to run."

She was trying to remain professional so she wouldn't endanger her business relationship with him. But it seemed as if everything she was saying now caused his features to harden a little more.

"If you bored me, do you honestly think I would have driven from St Hippolyte to be here with you this early in the morning?"

Heat rushed to her cheeks. She averted her eyes, not knowing what to believe. All she knew was that by some miracle her hope of spending time with him this trip had just been granted. She never wanted it to end.

"The truth is, I already knew some of the Alsatian wines were excellent. But I have to admit it was my grandfather who put the idea in my head to come here."

"The one who started the restaurants to honor his wife?" Luc interjected.

Rachel couldn't have been more surprised. "Yes—how did you know about that?"

"I told Philippe to do some homework for me so I could better serve you."

Rachel had had no idea Luc had gone to those lengths. No wonder he hadn't asked her a lot of questions about the family business last night. He hadn't needed to because his secretary had done it for him.

He left nothing to chance. The knowledge made him even more remarkable in her eyes.

"My grandfather has been ill. About three weeks ago he asked me to go through an old trunk for him and sort out his memorabilia.

"I'm making a journal of his life, so I was excited to see old letters and pictures he'd kept.

"When I handed him some photos to identify, I learned things I'd never known before. He heard I was leaving for France on another wine-buying trip, and urged me to come to Thann to look up an old French friend he'd met in Italy during the Second World War. Apparently they lost track of each other in the intervening years."

"*Ah, oui?*" Giles spoke up. "What was his name?"

"Louis Delacroix."

Giles smacked his forehead with his palm. "*Sacré bleu*— Louis? Did you hear that, Luc?"

"I did," her host murmured, staring at her with a strange new light in his eyes that made her legs grow weak.

"Louis was a good friend of mine," Giles explained, "but he died of pneumonia four years ago. Before he became ill, he went to live with his younger sister in Ribeauville."

Rachel was crushed by the news. "Oh, I'm sorry, not only for your loss, but for my grandfather's. He was eager to talk to him and reminisce about the old days. I have pictures I brought with me."

The older man's eyes dimmed for a moment. "Many of us from Thann were in the war. Not everyone came back, but Louis did."

"So did you, thank goodness. It was Louis who told Grandfather that Alsace produced the best white wine in the world. Of course my grandmother Lucia argued that Italian wine was better.

"Grandfather asked me to look him up so he could tell me which vintner in the region made the best white wine. After what you've told me, I have no doubt it was Chartier.

"When I couldn't find any 'Delacroix's listed in the phone directory, I asked the hotel concierge his opinion. He told me the Domaine Chartier."

"You've made our day," Luc declared in a husky voice. "Hasn't she, Giles?"

"Mais oui!" The news had caused the old man's expression to brighten again. "Your coming here is incredible!" he admitted.

Rachel found it pretty unbelievable too.

"I tell you what, Mademoiselle Valentine. Tomorrow we will drive to Ribeauville and pay Louis's sister a visit."

"Could we?" she cried eagerly. "Do you think she'd be willing to talk to my grandfather on the phone?"

He lifted his hands in a typical French gesture. "She will talk until his ear drops off."

While Rachel laughed, Luc said, "I have an even better idea, Giles. While you make arrangements with Solange for tomorrow, I'll take care of Ms Valentine today. We'll tour the vineyards and *en route* she can sample the wines you picked out for her. I'll get in touch with you later."

"Parfait." Giles packed the bottles in a carton. "I'll put this out in the car for you."

After he left, Luc's gaze trapped hers. "How does that plan sound to you?"

Though a little voice in her head warned her not to read too much into this, another part of her was screaming to go with him.

She moistened her lips, feeling a sudden nervous excitement over being with this arresting man who by some magic had caused her to abandon common sense.

"If you're sure."

He flicked her a questioning glance. "What's going on in that intelligent mind of yours?"

It could never be as brilliant as his. She had to think fast not to give her deepest reservation away.

"When my grandfather recovers, I'm going to bring him to Thann. Since he and Giles were friends with Louis, I'd like the two of them to meet. They're both remarkable people."

"Agreed. Otherwise your relative wouldn't have such a kind and compassionate granddaughter worrying about him. Every grandfather should be so lucky."

Stop saying these things to me, Luc. Already her attraction to him was too strong. If she were wise, she would leave for Champagne before the day was out.

"Thank you for the compliment, but the truth is, he's easy to love. Much as I'd like to phone him with this news right now, I'll wait and let Solange surprise him. A call from her will mean a lot more to him."

"That's a moment I would like to witness."

In an unexpected move, he cupped her elbow. "Shall we go?" His touch sent fingers of awareness through her. She was afraid he could feel her trembling.

Together they walked outside the convent, but she didn't understand when he led her to her car instead of his estate wagon.

"Follow me to the rental agency. After we drop off your car, I'll help you check out of your hotel. By the end of the day we'll get you installed in a hotel renowned in the region."

She shook her head. "You don't have to go to all this trouble for me."

"I like to take care of my potential buyers."

He opened the car door so she could climb inside. She took the greatest care to make sure her skirt wouldn't ride up her thighs, but before he shut the door his all-seeing glance took in everything anyway.

He leaned in the open window. "Have you forgotten that without wine buyers like you, I wouldn't have a business?"

That was true.

To her chagrin she'd been so mesmerized by him, she'd almost forgotten she was a woman who fell into the client category.

But *he* hadn't.

CHAPTER THREE

ON THE outskirts of Ribeauville, Rachel turned her head in Luc's direction.

"You live in the most beautiful place on earth." She drew in a deep breath of the warm June air. "Alsace must be one of the world's best kept secrets."

They'd long since checked her out of the hotel and had turned in her car.

The rest of the time she'd been drinking in the passing scenery while Luc gave her a history of the area. He'd enchanted her with a tale of the legend of Thann called the Miracle of the Fir Trees. She could listen to him indefinitely.

He darted her a lingering glance. "At the risk of sounding smug, I admit I feel the same way. I never wanted to be anywhere else but here, or do anything else except the work my father did."

"How wonderful to have that kind of relationship with him."

"I was very fortunate." His arm rested across the back of the seat, as if he needed more room to breathe and relax. His fingers grazed her shoulder. The slightest touch from him whether deliberate or not filled her with yearnings she couldn't tamp down.

"Tell me something—how is it you became so interested in wine, you turned it into a career?"

She stirred in her seat. "Unlike you I floundered over what I wanted to do with my life. I ended up with a college degree in communications, but I was no better off than before. For a graduation present Grandfather took me to Italy with him on a wine-buying trip.

"We met a blind vintner confined to a wheelchair from birth. He'd never been outside of Umbria, yet he knew about wines from all over the world.

"When I asked him how he'd learned so much, he said it wasn't necessary to travel to know about a place. All he had to do was drink the wine to know where it came from, and he was instantly transported there."

"That's true enough," said the striking man seated next to her.

"It comforted me to know that he didn't allow his disabilities to prevent him from living a full life. The more I thought about what he'd told me, the more I was challenged to try my hand at it, too. He never knew it, but he, along with Grandfather, were the two people responsible for my developing an uncommon interest in wines.

"Grandfather was a brilliant restaurateur. Between him and my grandmother, I was encouraged to learn all I could about the wines they liked the most."

"You've inherited his genes. I sensed that unique quality about you right away. You're a natural at this business."

"Coming from you that really means something. Thank you."

She closed her eyes tightly for a moment because this man was getting to her until she didn't know herself any more.

"It's only the truth."

She turned her head and stared out the passenger window so he couldn't see how emotional she'd become.

"While I was driving along these mountains yesterday, I could have wept for that vintner because he couldn't see the vineyards below the towering peaks I was seeing.

"He's no longer alive, but if he were I'd describe this place to him. I had no idea such beauty existed."

A palpable silence followed her remark as they climbed higher into the foothills above the town. Little by little civilization was left behind. From the window she could look down on an isolated castle, or a cluster of houses built around a quaint church.

Everywhere else the landscape was polka-dotted with *terroirs* forming their own unique mosaics.

At the top of the next crest she saw a small Black-Forest-type house sitting on the edge of its own little vineyard probably no bigger than three acres.

Though it blended with the other half-timbered houses she'd seen on the lower hillsides, she glimpsed remnants of building materials, indicating it was still under construction.

To her surprise he slowed down and pulled up in front of a detached two-car garage.

Rachel got out, moving slowly because she was so overcome by the fantastic view. It was hard to find words.

"I feel like I'm in a dream and nothing's real. This kind of beauty hurts."

She felt his presence behind her. "I knew you'd say that," he murmured in a thick-toned voice.

"Anyone would!" she exclaimed.

"No. Only someone with a sensitive nature like yours."

Rachel could scarcely credit he was talking to her this way.

Struggling to remember why she was here, she turned to him. "Does that mean you don't bring all your potential buyers to this spot?"

His eyes played over her upturned face for a breathtaking moment.

"No," came the one-syllable response, filling her with a kind of euphoria that seemed to be part of the day.

"It's been a long time since I met someone who relates to her surroundings on the emotional level you do. Being with you causes me to appreciate my world all over again. Does that make any sense to you?"

"Yes. Grandfather once told me God gave him grandchildren so he could relive his happy childhood through their eyes."

One dark eyebrow quirked. "I hardly see you as a child," he said in a wry tone.

"I think you know what I meant." She eyed him directly. "How long have you been divorced?" The question had left her mouth before she could stop it.

He didn't move a muscle, but she watched shadows chase away the amusement that had lit his eyes for a brief moment.

"Three years."

Unlike her father, who jumped in and out of marriage without counting the cost, this man had hidden depths that tempered him.

"I'm sorry for your pain, *monsieur*."

He shifted his weight. "My name is Luc. Is that so difficult for you to say?"

Her heart raced too fast. "I've been wanting to," she confessed, "but the French 'u' is a particularly difficult vowel sound for me to make." Her tongue kept running away with her. She enjoyed being with him too much.

"I'm afraid I speak two forms of English, so to say Luc, and make that pure sound correctly, will require some practice."

She felt his low, exciting chuckle reverberate around her insides.

"I'm impressed you work as hard at your French as you do your profession. Which part of you is American, Rachel?" She loved the way her name sounded falling from those French lips.

"My mother was from New York."

"She's passed away, then."

"Yes," Rachel said quietly.

"My father died two years ago. You never stop missing them."

"That's true. At least you have Giles, who appears to love you like one of his sons."

"It works both ways. I'm still learning about grapes from him. Is your father alive?"

"Oh, yes."

She saw the question in his eyes. "You're close?"

"He manages one of the restaurants, so we see each other pretty constantly. But after four marriages, he's not exactly capable of forming close relationships with anyone. In fact—"

She stopped mid-sentence, wishing she hadn't divulged something so personal. What was wrong with her?

"Go on," he urged.

"No. My family's problems aren't for anyone else's ears." She gazed at the surroundings. "What kind of grapes are these?"

"Sylvaner."

"Ah."

His lips relaxed in a half-smile. "So tell me what you know about them."

"If this is another test, I'll inform you right now I'm going to fail it."

"Be brave and humor me."

She closed her eyes. "Sylvaner is fresh—fruity—dry—young— How am I doing?"

When there was no answer, she opened them a little to peer up at him. It was a mistake. The way he was staring at her mouth erased every thought from her mind but one.

He'd gone perfectly still. "You left out spicy."

"That's right," she half moaned in frustration. "There's so much to learn."

"For someone who wasn't raised in a vintner's family, you know a great deal already and receive highest marks, Rachel."

Every time he said her name in his heavy accent, it made her forget what they were talking about.

He put his hands on his hips and looked out on the steep vineyard. "It *is* a young wine, which I'm trying to improve. I decided to build a house up here and use this vineyard for a laboratory."

"I can understand why. It's inspiring just to be in this heavenly spot away from distractions."

He nodded. "From the time I was old enough to follow my father around, it has been a favorite spot.

"In my teens, this vista made me feel master of all I surveyed. Lately it represents a place where I can be strictly alone. No one tends these vines but me."

"And now you have a house. How soon will it be finished?"

"Aside from a few things to still move in, it's done."

This was the kind of retreat she'd envisioned for herself. The type she hoped to buy one day. But this one wouldn't be on the market.

She looked away, tortured by another impossible dream where she lived in it with him.

It had been wrong of her to feel excitement when he'd told her he was no longer married.

What kind of a person was she to be happy about that piece of news when divorce was such a traumatic experience?

He must have loved his ex-wife very much not to have re-married yet.

His deepest feelings for her would explain the mysterious silences, his brooding aura at times.

Divorce had been the major cause of her pain growing up. The result being that she and her sister found themselves on opposite sides of a horrendous family tragedy.

She would always grieve that she hadn't been with her mother at the end, and that she didn't have a close relationship with Rebecca.

Too many years her family had been torn apart by their father's inability to stay with one woman and be happy.

Smoothing the hair off her forehead, she said, "You're a lucky man to be able to build your own place away from everyone."

"I take it you live in the heart of busy London."

She nodded. "A flat at Grey's Lodge I purchased several years ago. It has turned out to be a good investment."

"Where is it exactly?"

"On the boundaries of Earl's Court, Fulham and Chelsea."

"A fashionable part of the city. One of my buyers owns a club there."

She nodded. "Lots of the best shops and clubs are nearby. But the main reason I chose it was because of its close proximity to the restaurant my father manages."

"Who manages the other two?"

"My uncle John and his son Dominic, but my grandfather William oversees everything."

"A true family business, just like mine. It can be a challenge at times."

"That's a discreet way of putting it."

"Well, there's been no bloodshed. At least not yet," he teased, but she couldn't summon an answering smile.

"What did I say, Rachel? You've gone quiet on me."

"When you can joke about your family, then you know everything's really all right. I'm afraid in my family—well, let's just say it's different."

"How different? Tell me."

She lifted troubled blue eyes to him. "You really want to know?"

"I wouldn't have asked otherwise," he mimicked her words of yesterday evening.

"My father and his half brother John have always been in competition for Grandfather's attention.

"John was the son of his first marriage, which failed. When John's mother died, he came to live with my grandfather and Lucia.

"Dad was two at the time and doted on. But his happy world crumbled when eight-year-old John arrived.

"Though Grandfather has kept a fairly tight rein on both of them, Dad has a wild side I try not to provoke. He's planning to take over the family business after Grandfather dies. But John has the same plan in mind. It's awful." Her voice shook.

"As a result, Dad prides himself on staying a step ahead of both of them in everything.

"He was upset when he found out I'd come to Alsace on an errand for Grandfather. He sees everything as a conspiracy. I love him, of course, but it's all very complicated because I adore my grandfather and—"

"And your father expects your exclusive loyalty," he inserted with a degree of understanding that surprised her.

"Yes."

When she returned home from this trip, she planned to surprise her dad with his favorite whiskey *and* some vintage wine from the Chartier *caves*.

Rachel had never tasted such wine before. Once her father had sampled both varietals from their vineyards, he'd be won over, too. But he wouldn't like the fact that it had been her grandfather's idea.

"I can relate," he said matter-of-factly. "I, too, have an uncle who was always jealous of my father's friendship with Giles. And I have a brother-in-law who feels slighted if I show any of my other managers preference."

"No wonder you come up here to escape. If I weren't tied to a specific place, I'd find a hideaway like this. The sun here is glorious.

"I can't imagine anything more wonderful than working with a plot of ground and watching things grow. It would make all that effort worthwhile."

She sensed he was about to say something personal when his cell phone rang. He frowned before pulling it from his pocket.

She watched him check the caller ID. In an instant, lines marred his handsome features.

"Excuse me for a minute, Rachel. I need to take this call." He walked a little ways off.

Please don't let it be too urgent, her heart cried. She couldn't bear it if anything interrupted them now.

A second later he turned to her. "Something important has come up. I'm afraid we have to go."

"Of course. I'm surprised you've been able to give me this much time."

Putting on her best face, she walked to the car and got in before he could help her.

When they were on their way down the mountain, he eyed her with a dark, brooding look.

"I'm sorry about this. Tomorrow morning I'll take you around to the *caves* in this region. You haven't tasted our Sylvaner and Pinot Blanc yet."

"Only if you can spare the time. As for today, I plan to concentrate on the wines Giles sent with us for me to sample."

Luc didn't answer right away, which meant his mind was already on something else.

"We're coming up on a *ferme-auberge* famous for its excellent local food. You'll be put in an upstairs room overlooking the farm where they'll serve you your meals. From the deck you gaze out on a sight that I have no doubt will make another lasting impression."

"That sounds lovely." She meant it, but, pleased as she was by his concern for her enjoyment, it meant he was going to leave her once more.

Here she'd just been getting used to the idea that they would spend the whole day together. Now it sounded as if she wouldn't be seeing him again until tomorrow.

It would mean another restless night waiting for him to come back.

Would that she didn't care. She wished she could view Luc with the same dispassion she did any other vintner she'd just done business with, instead of...of...

Filled with disappointment, she closed her eyes knowing she would have been better off not to have come with him today.

Strengthening her resolve to keep distance between them, she made a promise to herself not to be this foolish a second time.

"Just in case this place is full, I can always stay at a small hotel down in the town."

At her words, she felt inexplicable tension emanate from him.

"My headquarters may be in St Hippolyte, but on any given day I have a standing arrangement with the owner to accommodate my buyers." Luc spoke in such an authoritative voice, Rachel gripped her purse a little tighter. She couldn't imagine what had brought on this remote side of him.

The owner of the half-timbered inn greeted Luc with a camaraderie of many years' standing, verifying Luc's claim.

The other man bid one of his staff to bring in her luggage and the carton of wines.

"Remy will take good care of you, Ms Valentine."

It wasn't *Rachel* any more?

Evidently Luc didn't want to risk giving his friend Remy the wrong impression of their relationship.

Or maybe Luc was warning her not to read more into today than the events deserved. Too many mixed signals were throwing her emotions into chaos.

He stared at her through veiled eyes. "Enjoy your stay."

Though he'd been perfectly civil in front of the other man, Rachel got the impression he was anxious to be gone.

Far be it from her to detain him. "Thank you, Monsieur Chartier. I'm sure I will."

There was a distinct pause while his enigmatic gaze focused on her hot cheeks. *"A demain."*

Rachel turned away from him to go upstairs.

See you tomorrow, he'd said.

Fine.

The moment she reached the rustic room built of rafters and floorboards from a bygone age, she changed into jeans and a knit top. After finding her walking shoes, she sat down on the dark four-poster to tie them.

Once that was accomplished she left the *auberge*.

Charming as her room was, she couldn't have remained in there or she would have gone a little crazy.

Hopefully on her walk through the countryside her mind would clear and she would regain the common sense she thought she'd been born with.

But as she made her way along one of the forest roads, she realized she was in trouble.

It was no use telling herself this was simply a strong physical attraction that would be forgotten once she left the area.

This time her emotions were involved even though it was too soon to be having these kinds of feelings for a man she barely knew.

When it happens, you'll know it, her grandfather had said.

Rachel was very much afraid she *did* know it.

"Sorry I'm late," Luc explained as he entered his attorney's office. "I couldn't get here any sooner."

It was close to three o'clock. Paul was probably due in court on some case. Luc hated holding him up.

The time he'd spent with Rachel today hadn't been nearly long enough. When he'd seen Paul's caller ID, Luc had been tempted to ignore it. But at the last minute he'd known he had to find out what was so important.

"I had to make hotel arrangements for a client who has come here on a buying trip."

The thought of not seeing her until tomorrow was a torment already eating at him.

"*Pas de problème,* Luc. It has given me time to go over some other cases." He removed his reading glasses to look at him.

"I thought you should know that the Brouets have gotten rid of their first attorney."

Luc stiffened. "What do you mean, first?"

"I'm getting to that. It appears they've hired a well known law-yer from Paris named Lebaux. He's had a lot of experience in these kinds of cases."

Luc's eyes held a far-away look. "If that's true, then they can't afford him."

Yves owned a computer store. His business was making a steady profit. That was good news for Luc's friend, who had a wife and two children to support.

But it killed Luc that Yves had probably contributed the most money in the Brouet family in order to pay for a high-pow-ered attorney.

"Nevertheless Lebaux has been retained and he has already brought the original court date forward with the judge for a pre-liminary hearing."

That meant Paulette's family had either gotten a loan from the bank, or they'd mortgaged their home to come up with the kind of funds required.

Fresh guilt pierced him.

"How soon?"

"The twentieth. That's this coming Monday. Two o'clock. I have to tell you honestly, Luc. It'll be a hard case for you to win."

"I'm aware of that."

"Still, you do have one thing that will let the judge know of your sincere desire for her full recovery. It's your unquestionable devotion to her for the last three years. No one can argue that you didn't love your wife, divorced or not."

Luc jumped up from the chair, stung because his thoughts since last evening had been centered on Rachel.

Today he'd found himself so attracted, he didn't want to en-tertain thoughts of her leaving Alsace.

It was one thing to feel desire for a near stranger he could slake with one passionate interlude before parting company. But it was quite another to imagine wanting this woman in his life.

When he thought back on his relationship with Paulette, his feelings for her had developed slowly over the years.

He couldn't relate to the man he was right now. Rachel's effect on him was a shocking reality he didn't know how to deal with because he felt a connection to her beyond the physical. How could it have happened this fast and hard while he was still fighting for Paulette to wake up?

He rubbed his neck in abject frustration and guilt.

"I appreciate what you're doing for me, Paul. I'll be in touch with you before the hearing."

"Hold on, Luc. We need to plan a new strategy. If you've got the time, let's do it now."

"I'm afraid I can't. I'm sorry." He knew himself too well. Something was happening to him. Someone had happened to him. He couldn't think clearly right now.

"*Bon*. The only other time I've got before Monday is tomorrow morning."

Tomorrow Luc was planning to spend the time with Rachel before he went to that damn banquet.

"What time do you want me here in the morning?"

"Ten o'clock. Is that all right?"

It would have to be. "Yes. Thanks, Paul. See you then."

After he left the law office, he headed straight to the hospital. The nurses on the afternoon shift nodded to him.

How many hundreds of times had he walked past them in the hope that they'd run after him with news that his ex-wife was coming around?

Before he reached her room, he heard the sound of the machines. They haunted him in his sleep.

He picked up the newspaper, his daily ritual, and began to read the day's events to her. After the headlines, he found articles on anything to do with fashion, travel and entertainment.

He stayed a couple hours before finally putting the paper aside.

"Paulette?" He reached for her hand, which he held between both of his.

"Have I made a mistake by hoping you'd wake up after all this time?

"Do you want this to be over? Everyone says you do. Yves is convinced of it. Maybe he knows something I don't. He loved you before I did.

"Tell me, *chérie*. I'm begging you to communicate with me. Heaven knows I don't want to do the wrong thing."

He waited for an answer as he did every time he spoke to her. None came.

In the final analysis, maybe no answer *was* his answer.

Kissing the back of her hand, he promised to return soon. When he left the hospital, he headed for his house.

Since his plans for tomorrow had to be changed, he needed to inform Rachel. But he intended to relay that information in person.

Before he did that, he needed a shower and shave.

It was after seven o'clock when Rachel returned from her long walk. She paused outside the window of the farmhouse's gift shop, marveling at the variety of souvenirs for sale.

When Luc had checked her in, she'd read the sign at the front desk. It said the family-owned inn had been operating for well over two hundred years.

No wonder there were so many unusual gifts to choose from. As she studied the items the dying rays of the sun illuminated several pieces of jewelry. Her interest was suddenly captured by the hand-painted porcelain pendant depicting three trees. It hung from a fine gold chain.

After the experience of hearing the Thann legend from Luc's lips, she had to have it in memory of the magical day she'd spent with him, even if it had been cut short.

Before she went up to her room for dinner, she decided to buy it now. The saleslady inside asked how she could help her.

"I'd like to see the pendant I noticed in the window."

The woman smiled. "You know about the Miracle of the Firs?"

"Yes. From someone very special."

"Just a moment and I'll get one from the back."

While Rachel waited, she wandered around until she came upon an Alsatian cookbook that was a first edition from the nineteenth century. She knew a certain chef who would love it. Without hesitation she pulled it from the shelf and carried it to the counter.

But another guest had gotten there ahead of her.

A certain tall, dark-haired male dressed in a dusky blue sport shirt and beige chinos, whose very presence had the power to turn her inside out.

Luc.

His bold gaze wandered up her jean-clad hips and body to her face, not missing a square inch of everything in between. He might just as well have set a torch to her.

"*Bonsoir,* Rachel."

Shock at seeing him here tonight rendered her speechless.

The saleslady reappeared behind the counter. "Here's the pendant you asked for. The green of the firs against the white background makes it a lovely piece of jewelry."

"I couldn't agree more," Luc concurred, sounding self-satisfied.

Rachel had not only been caught looking disheveled, she'd been caught in the act of making this particular purchase. It gave Luc tangible proof that his time spent with her had made an impact.

His eyes held a heart-pounding gleam. "Let me put it on you."

In a lightning move, he took it from the satin-lined box and stepped behind Rachel to place it around her neck.

He smelled wonderful. *He* was wonderful, and exuded too much sex appeal.

When he lifted her hair to fasten it, she swayed from the sensation of his hands against her hot skin.

"She'll take it," he told the woman, "and the book." Before Rachel could credit it, he'd drawn it from her arm and had put it on the counter.

"No, Luc—I'll pay for everything," she cried. His gesture had brought her out of her dream-like state, but it was no use. Ignoring her, he reached for his wallet and handed his credit card to the woman.

Rachel knew better than to make a scene. Later when they were alone, she would repay him.

The woman put the book and box in a bag.

After taking possession of it, he ushered Rachel into the lobby as if it were perfectly natural to treat her as if they were a couple.

The second she felt his hand grip her arm, the contact made her breath catch.

He steered her toward the staircase.

"Remy is sending up something special for our dinner. I don't know about you, but I haven't eaten all day and now I'm starving."

Rachel was feverish over this unexpected opportunity to be with him. In fact she felt close to a faint. If he hadn't been supporting her once they started up the stairs, she would have embarrassed them both by falling.

Her room was midway down the second-floor hall.

She fumbled in her purse for the key, which he took from her hand and inserted in the lock.

He opened the door, then waited for her to enter before shutting it behind them.

For one hysterical moment she wished he were her bridegroom, and he'd just carried her over the threshold to start their new life together.

But she wore no wedding ring, only the pendant he'd bought for her.

"If you'll excuse me for a moment, I'll freshen up."

"Take your time, Rachel. I'm in no hurry now."

Her limbs trembling in reaction, she hurried into the bathroom to brush her hair and put on fresh lipstick.

One look in the mirror confirmed her suspicions.

Her cheeks were flushed and her eyes shone like the love-struck woman she'd become since being around him.

The pendant drew her gaze. With the memory of what had gone on in the gift shop still fresh in her mind, she needed to do something so he wouldn't read too much into it.

After undoing the clasp and leaving it on the counter, she entered the living room. A quick glance around and she saw that he'd opened the double doors leading to the deck containing a table and chairs. She had to remember he'd probably entertained dozens of clients like this before.

Taking advantage of the moment, she opened her purse and signed one of her traveler's checks.

Filled with purpose, she walked across the room to join him. He darted her a quizzical glance when she extended him the check.

He made no move to take it. In fact a grimace stole over his attractive features because he'd noticed she'd removed the pendant.

"Keep your money, Rachel."

"Under other circumstances, I would," she said quietly. "However, I bought the pendant for my twin sister, Rebecca. A peace offering, if you like, in the hope that another miracle might happen one day."

Though she'd made that story up on the spur of the moment, she realized she wanted to buy a second one to send her sister.

He looked surprised. "I didn't know you had a full sibling. Are you identical?"

"No."

She would have said more but there was a tap on the door.

"I'll get it."

Luc's well-honed physique moved past her to let the waiter in.

The younger man pushed the teacart through to the deck. Luc slipped him a tip and saw him out.

Rachel put the check in her pocket, then busied herself putting their food on the table.

Luc approached carrying a bottle of wine from the carton.

"The main course we're going to eat tonight is best enjoyed with this particular vintage of our Riesling."

They were both still standing as he opened it and poured the pale liquid into their wineglasses.

He handed one to her. His slumberous gaze didn't leave her face.

"To Rachel Valentine, Bella Lucia's finest ambassadeuse."

She shouldn't have been cut to the quick by his reference to her professional status, but she was…

To make certain he didn't get the wrong idea about her feelings, she clinked his glass with hers.

"To Louis Delacroix, who is ultimately responsible for the Chartier wines that will grace our tables in future."

She thought Luc would say, *"Touché,"* but he didn't. That pleased her.

She took a quick swallow without tasting it, and sat down so he wouldn't come near her.

If he drank more of his wine, she didn't watch.

Maybe other women could handle a situation like this without getting burned. Unfortunately Rachel didn't know the rules.

Was Luc playing a game with her?

Some moments she could swear he wasn't toying with her. Yet in the next breath he said something that knocked the foundation out from under her, leaving her uncertain and more vulnerable than she'd ever been in her life.

"How do you like your meal?" he inquired after a few minutes.

"It's delicious. So is the wine." She refused to meet his eyes.

"Does your sister live in London too?"

Now that she'd told him the jewelry was for Rebecca, he wasn't about to leave the subject alone.

"No. New York, and everywhere else her advertising job takes her."

A tension-filled silence followed.

"Rachel—what have I said that has upset you so much?"

The concern in his deep voice defeated her. She wiped the corner of her mouth with her napkin.

"It's nothing to do with you, Luc," she lied. "I'm sorry if I gave you that impression."

"Then this has to be about your sister."

"Yes." She seized on the kernel of truth he'd thrown her. "We haven't been close in years. I don't know how to fix it."

"What happened to cause the breach between twins?"

Unbidden tears stung her eyes.

Damn.

"I—I wasn't there when Mother died. I loved her desperately, and I should have gotten there in time, but I was on business wi— Oh—it doesn't matter what the reasons were that delayed me. The fact remains I got there too late and Rebecca has never forgiven me.

"No matter how many times Grandfather has told me it wasn't my fault, I've never been able to forgive myself.

"He says the only thing I've done wrong is not allowing myself to get over this and move on. But how do you throw off that kind of guilt?" she cried before she realized what a fool she was making of herself. What was she doing pouring her heart out to a man she'd only met twenty-four hours ago? It didn't make any sense!

Luc looked at her with too much compassion. She couldn't handle it.

"Forgive me for breaking down in front of you," she said in a dull voice. "I can't believe I did that."

"Don't apologize. I'm flattered that you felt comfortable enough with me to let go of your emotions."

She sensed a pause before he said, "We all suffer from our own brand of demons."

No doubt he was speaking from experience. Divorce left its scars.

"Maybe, but yours couldn't possibly be as bad as mine."

When he didn't say anything, she worried she'd touched a nerve and hurried to cover her gaffe. "The dynamics of the Valentine family are very complicated, but I've already told you that."

His hand unexpectedly grasped hers across the table. "No matter how much you may have suffered inwardly, all I see is a successful, confident woman. I admire you for that more than you know, Rachel."

He squeezed her fingers before letting them go.

"Thank you." She lifted her eyes to his. "From my vantage point, your demons don't appear to have affected your performance either. You have unmatchable status in a country that prides itself on producing the world's greatest wines. It's a privilge to know you, Luc."

He eyed her through shuttered lids. "You sound like you're giving a goodbye speech. I'm still here if there's more you'd like to talk about."

Oh, Luc— He could have no idea how much she wanted to take him up on his offer.

But because she didn't know where it would lead, she needed him to go. One false step could take her beyond the point of no return.

"Thank you, but I happen to know your work requires you to be up at the crack of dawn. If we're going to visit your vineyards in the morning, we both need our sleep."

His expression sobered. He scrutinized her features as if trying to decide how best to tell her something she wasn't going to like.

No—

Not again—

But his next words confirmed her worst fears.

"Something's come up that I didn't know about until I met with my attorney this afternoon."

That explained why he'd come to the farmhouse tonight.

"He's working on a case for me which requires another work session in the morning. Following that I have a vintner's banquet I can't get out of because I'm one of the featured speakers."

"You don't have to explain. I understand you have obligations. Please don't be concerned about me."

His dark brows formed a bar of displeasure. "You came all this way on business and deserve full service for your time. Under the circumstances I'll leave you in Giles' hands and meet up with you later in the day when I'm free of commitments."

She schooled her features not to reveal her dejection.

"Only if it's convenient," she said, following him to the door.

Her comment seemed to irritate him further. "Get a good sleep, Rachel."

"How could I do anything else in such a beautiful place?" She flashed him a smile she didn't feel.

"I enjoyed this evening very much,"

"So did I."

"The Riesling was superb."

He didn't appear to hear her, yet she sensed he was reluctant to leave. Or maybe that was just wishful thinking on her part.

What if she begged him to stay a little longer? Would he do it?

If she gave in to that temptation, would he consider it an invitation to stay for the whole night and think less of her?

Somewhere in all this she had to preserve her dignity and think about her career.

Naturally she wasn't so naïve that she didn't recognize he found pleasure in her company. She could tell from his eyes that he thought she was attractive.

Yet she had to remember he met fascinating women from every walk of life all the time. What was one more to him?

She'd sell her soul to know how he really felt about her. But she simply couldn't risk his disapproval if she made a wrong move.

After a battle between desire and reason, she chose the latter.

"Goodnight, Luc."

"A tout à l'heure," he finally whispered before disappearing out the door, taking her heart with him.

CHAPTER FOUR

BY THE time Luc left his house for St Hippolyte the sun had gilded his vineyard with morning light.

He hoped to catch up with Yves before his friend left for work. Ten minutes later he turned on Yves' street and was relieved to see his green car still parked out in front.

No doubt he and Camille were up with the children.

Luc would have come by last night if it hadn't been so late. This morning nothing could have stopped him.

Meeting Rachel had changed him in ways he wouldn't have believed.

These new feelings of exhilaration weren't some fleeting reaction that would die once she went back to England.

Mon Dieu—he didn't want her going anywhere.

He needed her here so they could explore what was happening between them. He knew in his gut they were happening to her, too.

In two days he'd become a different person. Being with her made it impossible for him to go back to that dark place where he'd only been existing for the last few years.

He pulled up up behind the other car, eager to talk to his friend. Yves was going to be shocked.

Shutting off the motor, Luc hurried up the steps to the front door and knocked. When Yves eventually answered and saw who it was, his eyes darkened in pain and confusion. Within seconds he stepped outside and shut the door, letting Luc know he wasn't welcome.

"*Tiens!* If you've come to make me see reason, you're too late!"

Luc deserved that. He stared hard at him. "I came here to tell you to call off Monsieur Lebaux."

Yves grimaced. "Not a chance in hel—"

"I'm not finished," Luc broke in. "All I ask for is the rest of the summer. If Paulette hasn't come out of her coma by then I'll know she wants to be free, as you said.

"Tell your family there's no need for litigation. You have my word on that."

He could see Yves was having difficulty swallowing. So was Luc.

"Something earth-shaking must have happened to you."

Luc nodded. "I've met someone. It's made me realize that everything you've tried to tell me is true."

A long silence followed. Then, "*Merci, Dieu,*" his friend whispered fiercely.

In a sudden movement he gave Luc a bear hug, the kind they'd shared at the wedding that had made them brothers through marriage.

It was the first spontaneous gesture of affection from Yves in a long while.

Luc hugged him back hard, not realizing until this minute how much he'd missed their camaraderie.

In truth he hadn't felt this close to him since the night Luc's father had died of heart failure and Yves had come to comfort him.

With the advent of Rachel in his life, he was discovering that he'd been dead to all feelings for such a long time, coming back to life was breathtakingly painful. And thrilling.

Rachel handed the last of her pictures to Solange. They were copies she could keep.

The cordial Frenchwoman spoke good English and was still active for being seventy-nine years old.

"As you can see, this is Grandfather and Louis at a café in Rome with Lucia."

"Ah," Solange cried. "She is very beautiful, like you. And look at Louis. So short, and your grandfather, so tall. Yet both are young and handsome!"

"They are," Rachel concurred. "If Grandfather is able to talk, would you be willing to say a few words? He'll want to hear anything you have to tell him about your brother."

"But of course!" she exclaimed.

This couldn't be going better. Rachel reached for her cell phone, but Solange's hands flew in the air.

"I don't like those phones. Use my land line."

"All right. I'll have the charges reversed."

Rachel picked up the receiver and dialed London. She was tickled when her grandfather answered right away. Mornings were his best time.

"Grandfather? It's Rachel. Are you free to talk, or are you still eating your breakfast?"

"It's always the right time when you call. Besides, I had my breakfast an hour ago."

She loved his positive outlook on life, but his voice sounded a little weak. "Then I'm going to put someone on the phone who will introduce herself."

"Herself?"

"Just a minute and all your questions will be answered."

She handed Solange the phone, then sat back in the chair to listen.

As they began to talk and exchange stories, the older woman's laughter and tears touched Rachel's heart. Her own eyes grew moist.

They must have gone on talking fifteen minutes before Rachel turned to Giles with a grateful smile. "Solange is wonderful."

He winked. "She thinks you are, too."

Another ten minutes and Solange handed her the phone. "Your grandfather wants to talk to you again."

Rachel took it from her. "Grandfather?"

"Rachel—" His voice sounded croaky. "You've made this old man very happy."

She sniffed. "I'm glad."

"Hurry home so I can see all the new pictures you've taken. Solange says she'll be sending some of Louis's that show me and your beautiful grandmother with him."

"I've been looking at them all morning. I promise to be back soon and we'll pore over them."

"That's my sweet gIRL—" His coughing was starting again.

"Hang up and drink some water. I love you."

Rachel put the receiver back on the hook, wishing he still didn't have that cough.

She reached for Solange's hand.

"Talking to you meant more to Grandfather than anything. Thank you for letting me come by this morning."

"It has been my pleasure. But won't you stay longer?"

"We can't," Rachel said before Giles could. "I have restaurant business to do back at the *auberge*. Giles has to take me there before he leaves for the vintners' banquet.

"But when my grandfather gets better, we'll come for a visit, and that's a promise."

"Good." She handed Rachel a packet of pictures to take with her. After they kissed on both cheeks, the three of them walked to the door and said goodbye.

It wasn't long before Giles dropped Rachel off in front of the farmhouse, assuring her Luc would be in touch later.

She gave him a big hug and thanked him for everything before hurrying inside.

"Rachel Valentine," she muttered when she entered her room. "Before things get any more complicated, it's time you dealt with a situation that's your problem, not Luc's."

Without hesitation she phoned her travel agent and arranged for a rental car to be delivered to the *auberge* straight away.

When she'd done that, she called the front desk for the number of Chartier et Fils.

After writing it down, she punched in the digits. To her relief, she reached a recording at Domaine Chartier, asking the caller to leave a message.

She waited for the beep, then improvised. "Monsieur Chartier? This is Rachel Valentine. Forgive me for disturbing you, but I've had an unavoidable change in schedule and must leave.

"I'll ask the owner of the *auberge* to fax my wine order to your office. Be assured I've arranged for an electronic transfer of funds.

"On behalf of Bella Lucia, I want to thank you and Giles Lambert for making this the most memorable experience of my buying trip to France."

A trip that needed to come to an end.

She hung up and got busy on her packing, which included several precious bottles of wine.

Before she went downstairs to check out, she came across the rental car brochure with its detailed map of France. The agency had given it to her when she'd first arrived in Colmar.

According to the information, the largest automobile museum in the world was located in Mulhouse, near Thann.

If she backtracked from St Hippolyte, she could purchase some miniature models from their gift shop before leaving the province.

Her father collected classic cars which he housed in an extended garage at his house in South Kensington.

Knowing him, he would put them on Bev's favorite glass coffee table held up by four gold elephants, just to get a rise out of her.

Another gift to pacify her father who could never be pacified for long.

Maybe Rachel was more like him than she knew. What could possibly satisfy her after she returned to the UK? The mere idea of leaving here, leaving Luc...brought such fierce pain she felt ill.

After taking his leave of Yves, Luc had given his short talk at the Alsatian vintners' banquet and was now in his car heading for his house. Once he'd changed out of his suit into something casual, he had plans for Rachel and himself.

Since she found the area so beautiful, he was looking forward to her reaction when he drove her to a special place he had in mind.

He'd never met anyone who took such genuine pleasure in everything. As if each moment was a great adventure. Luc had to admit he was intrigued by that childlike quality in her woman's mind and body.

With his thoughts so immersed in Rachel, he did a double take to see his mother coming out of his house as he drove up.

She walked toward him. *"Bon après-midi, mon fils.* I thought you'd still be at the banquet, so I took advantage of the time to bring you a little food for tonight."

"Thank you, *Maman*, but I don't expect this to become a habit, *tu comprends?*"

She did too much. He understood why, but it had to stop.

"Can't a mother do something for her son?" she chided him affectionately.

"By the way, there was a message on the office answering machine. Giselle said it just came in from a Ms Valentine. I didn't realize you'd been doing business with a buyer from London."

His body stilled. "Giles has been taking care of her. What did her message say?"

"Something came up, forcing her to leave the area. But she faxed you a very large order, and—"

"Forgive me, *Maman*, but I have to go."

He put his car in gear and backed out to the road. There was no time to waste. Something had gone on since Giles had dropped Rachel off, otherwise she would have said something to the old man.

Yesterday Luc had felt out of control. As for today...

If he could be this upset at her leaving, how would he feel to get truly involved and then lose her the way he'd lost Paulette?

Maybe it was better that he let her walk away now, before it was too late.

But even as he reasoned that way, his foot pressed the accelerator to the floor, sending the Wagoneer barreling down the mountain.

Knowing Rachel, she'd rented a car. But whether she was on her way to Champagne, or had left for Colmar to catch a flight back to the UK, was anyone's guess.

Before he called her cell, he phoned to retrieve her message.

Unfortunately it told him nothing about her itinerary.

Letting go with an expletive, he punched the digit where he'd stored her phone number.

After two rings he was told to leave a message.

His hand almost crushed his phone before he made a call to Remy.

The other man couldn't help him out except to tell him she'd left in a Monde Français rental car.

Monde Français.

Luc's friend Georges worked there. He would tell Luc what he needed to know.

Rachel switched the cell phone to her other ear.

"Can you hear me better now, Emma?"

Her half sister was always in the kitchen in the afternoon. As she was the head chef at Bella Lucia, it was the best time to reach her. The rest of the day would find her too busy.

"A little. Go on. What were the ingredients after the scallops and sauerkraut?

"Add some grilled bacon and a sauce of clotted cream with a touch of herbs and Chartier Riesling."

"That sounds interesting."

"Last night I had one of the best meals I've ever eaten in my life. I thought you might like to experiment with it. It won't taste the same without the Chartier label, of course, but at least it will give you the idea.

"I'm bringing you and Max back a bottle of the real thing. If you love the recipe as much as I do, you might want to add it to the menu. Their wine is to die f—"

Rachel broke off talking because someone behind her was honking.

"Just a minute, Emma."

She pulled closer to the edge so the other car could pass. But when it started to go around her, she realized it was staying right alongside her.

Irritated, Rachel shot the driver a speaking glance. But when she saw who it was, she experienced *déjà vu* and almost ran off the road.

"E-Emma?" her voice faltered. "I'll have to call you back."

Dropping the phone, she grabbed the steering wheel with both hands and came to a stop at the side of the road as soon as she could.

While traffic passed by, Luc pulled directly behind her and through the rear-view mirror she saw this gorgeous male lever himself from the car.

Maybe he was the prince she'd envisioned when she'd seen him at the base of the convent. But this prince wore a modern-day blue suit with a white shirt and tie.

As he drew closer her mouth went so dry she couldn't swallow.

He tapped on the window while she fumbled with the switch before it finally lowered. The heat had grown intense, forcing her to turn on the air-conditioner.

He trapped her gaze. "When I heard you had a sudden change in plans, I felt impressed to catch up with you and see if there's anything I can do to help. Has something happened to your grandfather?"

She tore her eyes from his, absolutely stunned he'd gone out of his way to track her down.

"How did you find me?"

"My friend works at the car rental."

He knew everyone and everything. This was exactly what she hadn't wanted to happen, at least not consciously.

"Grandfather was all right when I talked to him earlier today." She struggled to come up with an excuse that wouldn't give her away.

"Actually I've stayed in Alsace longer than I'd planned. Now my business is done here."

"*Maman* told me you placed a large order. I can't complain about that, now, can I? But I'm still waiting for the answer to my question."

"I'm supposed to be in Châlons-Sur-Champagne today."

Ignoring her declaration, he said, "I noticed you talking on the phone. If you have a boyfriend who has become impatient for your return, then your action is understandable."

"No—" she blurted. "That's not the reason."

He had to know she wasn't interested in anyone else.

Judging by his ghost of a smile, her denial appeared to have pleased him.

"Since you were aware of your business plans before you came to Alsace, then I believe I know the real reason you chose to slip away this afternoon, but we can't discuss it here. Follow me into Thann. We're almost there now."

"Wait, Luc. Please listen to me —"

But he'd already started for his car.

By the time her trembling limbs could function enough to put the car in gear, he started passing her. As he drove by she felt his dark brown gaze probing hers. She knew if she didn't follow him, he'd be back to find out why.

Her pounding heart almost suffocated her before she pulled onto the road behind him.

Much as she knew this was wrong, her emotions had taken over, crowding out her misgivings.

He'd said he knew the reason for her abrupt departure. She couldn't imagine how he knew, but at least they were going to talk, It was something she'd been craving since last night. This time he wasn't hurrying off to meet another deadline. Just the opposite, in fact.

It had been such a wrench to leave this afternoon without seeing him again, she'd phoned Emma in order to hold on to what little sanity she had left.

Emma—

Rachel would have to call her back, but not right now. She couldn't think. All she was capable of doing was keeping him in her sights.

Before long she realized the convent was his destination.

This time he took a circuitous route through a forested area of the estate. The private road wound through the underbrush until it came out on another courtyard where she glimpsed a rectangular swimming pool.

With the temperature of the air still rising, the blue water looked divine.

Luc parked his car and walked over to her.

"Before we do anything else, let's cool off, shall we?"

"I didn't bring a swimming costume with me."

"That's not a problem. Giselle and I both have apartments here. You can use her room. I believe you'll find everything you need in one of the big chests."

That explained how he'd changed out of his suit into casual clothes the first night they'd met.

He opened her door so she could slide out from behind the wheel. Before she knew it, he'd reached for her cases.

"This is a fabulous place, Luc."

They walked toward a door he unlocked with a remote from his pocket.

"There's a lot of history here. Giselle and I have always liked it. Years ago she staked out the mother superior's room. It's larger than the cells once used by the professed nuns."

Rachel chuckled. "You didn't mind?" she asked as he led her into a shadowy corridor with doors on both sides. They climbed the stone steps to the next floor.

"Not with this pool right outside. In the summers the parents would stay here. After they went to bed, Yves and I used to sneak in our friends.

"Of course the parents knew all about it. *Maman* would pretend to be shocked, but we always found food waiting when we raided the kitchen in the middle of the night."

"How fun for you."

"Our childhood was pretty idyllic."

"That's the way every child's should be."

Their eyes met in silent understanding.

He opened a door on the left. Rachel peeked inside and let out a soft gasp.

With the exception of a modern queen-sized bed, the interior looked very much the way it must have done in the fourteen hundreds.

"Oh, Luc—"

She didn't think anything could eclipse this sight until she glanced at him and felt the full brunt of his captivating white smile.

He lowered her cases to the inlaid hardwood floor.

"There'll be plenty of time for you to take pictures—" he read her mind "—but first things first.

"We have a rule around here. The last one in the pool will have to pay the consequences."

"And what might those be?"

"You'll find out."

"So you think you're going to win?"

A devilish gleam entered his eye. It sent her flying across the room to the chests he'd referred to.

Within seconds she found a drawer with half a dozen bikinis.

She grabbed the most modest one she could find. It was blue with tiny pink flowers that looked as if it would fit. Then she hurried into the *en suite* bathroom to change.

Hoping it was all right to use one of the bath towels, she rushed back down the stairs with it and opened the heavy door to the courtyard.

"No—" she screamed because Luc was already there dressed in black trunks waiting for her.

"Please, no—" But her frightened laughter and cries went ignored. His powerful arms and body fought off her puny struggles.

"In you go, ready or not." Merciless to the end, he carried her to the deep area of the pool. But instead of dropping her like a hot potato, he took them both to the bottom.

The sensation of their legs and bodies intertwined with bubbles was more intoxicating than the Riesling she'd drunk with him last night. She scarcely noticed the cold water.

In reality it wasn't cold, but Luc had created a fever inside of her. She felt like a fireworks sparkler that was sizzling beneath the surface of the water.

His dark eyes danced as she popped above the surface.

"Oh, no—my towel—" She could see it floating beyond his broad shoulders.

"You don't need it," he murmured.

They trod water together. Her eyes traveled to his dark brown hair sleeked back to reveal his handsome features.

The late afternoon sun bronzed his olive skin.

"You look like the off-duty captain of a pirate ship," she teased to cover her emotions.

He burst into deep laughter. The joyous kind.

That remote, aloof side of his nature he sometimes displayed had gone into hiding. She wanted him to stay this way for ever.

"You look like the woman on the masthead of my ship come to life at my whim."

Afraid he could see her blushing, she somersaulted away from him and headed for the side of the pool.

He was right at her heels, cleaving the water in a few long, masterful strokes.

She reached for the tiled edge. When she turned around, there he was, inches from her.

His eyes followed the line of her lips. "Before I have to be back on duty, my one desire is to taste my private treasure."

So saying, he placed his hands on either side of her and lowered his mouth to hers.

Rachel had wanted this for so long, she met the pressure of his mouth with shocking urgency.

She'd kissed and been kissed by different boyfriends over the years, but this was different. So completely different it frightened her because she knew she'd never be the same again.

Her whole being felt swallowed up in him. While he drove their kiss deeper and deeper, she forgot they weren't one flesh of heart-throbbing need.

She made a little moan of protest when he lifted his mouth.

"Now that we have that out of the way," he said on a ragged breath, "tell me why you ran from me today."

She couldn't meet his eyes. "I didn't run."

"No?" he demanded. In the space of a millisecond his mood had changed. She edged further away from him.

It was the wrong thing to do. He just moved in closer so their bodies brushed against each other in the water.

He put his hand beneath her chin and lifted it so she was forced to face him. "I don't know what else you'd call it."

"I—I felt I'd become a nuisance," she stammered. "Normally I make plans to visit a vintner several months in advance. But in your case I arrived unannounced. You've had to make all sorts of accommodations for me. Poor Giles—"

"Poor Giles has been having the time of his life," Luc cut her off.

"So have I," she confessed. "I've learned reams about wine from him. In my opinion he's a national treasure."

Disarming laughter broke from him once more.

"An apt description of Giles. I can't wait to tell him."

"He and Solange are both terrific individuals."

"I couldn't agree more. It's a small world when a stranger comes to Thann and ends up brightening the lives of two people who love to live in the past."

She made the mistake of looking at him. "You've just described my grandfather. He always tells me he feels sorry for me because I didn't live in the golden age following World War II."

He held her glance. "My grandparents said the same thing to me. Each generation thinks theirs is incomparable."

She nodded. "I suppose it is to them."

"But you don't feel that way about your life?"

Rachel bit her bottom lip. "I don't know. I haven't lived all of it yet."

"*Touché*," he murmured in such an odd tone she trembled a little.

Though they were talking on one level, something else was happening on another. She had a premonition they weren't making idle conversation any more.

Without warning he heaved himself from the water, then extended his hands to pull her out.

"Let's get dressed and drive into town. I know a little place that serves pasta Alsacienne style."

His moods changed so fast, she couldn't keep up with him.

"That sounds good."

Except that she wasn't hungry, not after trying to keep up with his mercurial emotions.

"Oh—the towel!"

"I'll get it later. Let's go."

He grasped her hand. They walked back inside the convent. Whatever was on his mind had to be serious. Maybe over dinner he would tell her.

CHAPTER FIVE

Luc ushered Rachel inside the Petit Vosges. The fragrance from her strawberry shampoo assailed him.

"I often come here with Giles after work. As you can see, it contains all sorts of memorabilia from the war years."

"It's amazing," she exclaimed. "I'll have to bring Grandfather when he gets better."

Luc was planning on it.

He ushered her to an empty table in the corner and motioned the waiter over.

"Do you trust me to order for you?"

Rachel's blue eyes fastened on him. They looked more brilliant in the candlelight against the leaf-green of her suit. She was so damn stunning, he couldn't take his eyes off her.

"Of course. In fact I'd prefer it."

He had to tear his attention away from her to order the scampi pasta and beer.

After the waiter walked away, a bewitching smile broke the corner of her mouth. An incredible mouth. The memory of that kiss had altered the rhythm of his heart.

"I understood your French, but I didn't know you liked beer."

"Only the draft on tap here. I'm curious to know how you'll like it, and the music."

Her expression livened. "What kind?"

"Are you familiar with Edith Piaf?"

"Yes. Grandfather said she was called the little French bird who sang her heart out during the war."

"That's true. The female vocalist who performs here looks and sounds incredibly like her. If you have a favorite song from the past, she'll sing it for us."

"I know Grandfather had one. It had something to do with the soldier who didn't come back."

Luc nodded. "I know the one."

"As I recall, it was very sad."

Rachel's voice sounded wistful just now, reminding him of what she'd said earlier about life.

I haven't lived all of it yet.

Those words had resonated in some secret part of him. That was because he hadn't lived all of it yet, either.

Being with her made him hunger for the things he'd thought were over. He needed to tell her, but he would wait for the right moment.

"The pasta is marvelous," she said a little while later.

"And the beer?"

"Well..." She made a little face that caused him to chuckle.

"It's all right if you don't like it, Rachel. I have to admit it's an acquired taste."

"How long did it take you?"

"To acquire it?" he questioned poker faced. "To be honest, I never really did."

"I *knew* it."

She leaned forward. Her eyes flashed blue sparks. "You're a purist, and a horrible tease. I bet your sister could tell me stories—"

Giselle would approve of Rachel. Luc knew that in his gut.

He was about to tell her so when the singing started.

Luc moved his chair around so he could put his arm on the back of Rachel's. He needed that closeness and the warmth of her body next to him.

For the next half-hour he found the greatest of pleasure watching the woman next to him enjoying the show. Especially when the vocalist performed Luc's request.

"Thank you for today," Rachel said later when he drove them back to the convent. "It's been unforgettable."

"That sounds like another goodbye speech."

Her head was bowed. "I really can't stay in Alsace any longer."

"What if I asked you to stay through the weekend? Since my divorce, I haven't wanted to be with another woman. Then... there you were."

He heard a little moan escape her throat.

"You must have loved her very much."

"I did. In fact I couldn't imagine moving on. But meeting you has made me realize life is full of possibilities.

"Think about it and tell me in the morning."

Before he made the mistake of rushing her, he got out of the car and went around to help her.

When he let her inside the convent, he held back from climbing the stairs with her.

"I'm going to do a few laps in the pool before bed. You go on. I can tell you're sleepy. Don't worry about anything. You'll be as safe as a nun tonight."

An hour later Rachel was still wide awake, no closer to deciding what to do than when she'd first slid beneath the covers.

She finally sat up and turned on the lamp to find her laptop.

Luc expected an answer in the morning. What tortured her was the knowledge that if she stayed, she'd be giving him her heart and soul.

But she couldn't say the same thing for Luc. If he'd been telling her the truth, and she was the first woman to interest him since his divorce, then he couldn't possibly be in the same place emotionally that she was.

Three days together might be all he wanted or needed from her. She couldn't risk playing with her life's happiness that way.

If they lived in the same city...

But they didn't.

Luc was a prominent man with a whole company looking to him for their livelihood. He couldn't come to England on a moment's notice.

Under the circumstances there was no way a lasting relationship could develop.

Heartsick, she needed something to occupy her mind, so she

brought up the file on her book. It made her feel closer to Luc. She could still hear his voice explaining everything in that unforgettable French accent.

"The dry wine of Alsace tends to have a fullness which provides a rich contrast from, say, the Mosel wines. Its fruity flavor goes especially well with food.

"Alsace's unique geological make-up is the reason for the exciting aromatic differences found nowhere else in the world."

Because of his knowledge and intelligence, being with him was a great thrill. All she had to do was say yes to his invitation and she could have three more days with him.

And then what? Never see him again?

Her body ached with pain. Luc had no idea he was the reason the book she planned to write was starting to take shape. Already a title had come to mind.

One day years from now, when she was brave enough to ask him to read the first draft and make suggestions, she would prevail on him to write the foreword.

In order to do that, she'd be wise not to get into deeper waters. If she said goodbye to him tomorrow, she could leave with the memory of that kiss, and still retain their professional friendship.

Letting out a tormented sigh, she put everything away and turned out the light again.

Before she finally fell asleep, her pillow became so waterlogged, she had to grab the other one.

She awakened in the morning in agony, but her mind was made up.

Determined to leave looking her best for him, she showered and applied a pink lipstick. Then she dressed in one of her favorite outfits, a sleeveless pinstripe dress in blue on white. The summery material was so light, it seemed to float around her legs.

She tied her hair back at the nape with a white ribbon, and slipped on white sandals. Once she was ready, she made up the room. After a look around to make certain she hadn't forgotten anything, she went downstairs with her cases.

Luc was already in the courtyard putting the last lounger from the pool away in a storage unit.

He was such a beautiful man, her heart pounded outrageously. It always did that at the first sight of him.

His dark head swiveled around, making eye contact with her.

He walked toward her looking amazing in jeans and a T-shirt that molded his powerful body, but there was no greeting from him.

She sensed immediately something was wrong.

"I had a feeling in my gut you might decide to leave without telling me."

His remark brought her up short. Her body stiffened. "I would never have done that." She spread her hands. "Luc—what's the matter?"

A somber expression marred his striking features. He grimaced. "Admit you were going to tell me you couldn't stay."

She held his fiery gaze. "Yes. I think it's for the best."

He would never know her pain, but she was fighting for her life.

His jaw hardened inexplicably. "If that's your wish, then I'll follow you to the Hotel du Roi in Thann where you can stay until tomorrow."

"Tomorrow? What do you mean?"

"I mean you can forget driving to Champagne or anywhere else today."

She blinked. "I don't understand."

His brows furrowed. "A storm alert has been issued. We don't often get electrical storms on this side of the Vosges, but when they come, they can be vicious."

His warning alarmed her. Not so much from his words, but the intensity with which he'd said them.

If her senses didn't deceive her, she'd heard a tone of real concern in his voice.

"You honestly think it could be that bad?"

His brown eyes turned black as jet. "In two thousand a ferocious storm wiped out thirty-five per cent of the trees in Alsace."

Her body shuddered at the thought of such terrible devastation.

"Look behind you if you need proof."

When she did his bidding, she could see dark thunderheads gathering in the far distance.

"I believe you. They look ominous."

"This whole area will be deluged through tomorrow. If you're not used to the conditions, you could find yourself in real trouble."

He honestly feared for her safety. She could feel it.

That meant she'd been given another day with him if she wanted it.

Heavens—*if* she wanted it—

Shifting restlessly, she said, "What about that plot of new vines at your vineyard? Will the storm destroy them?"

His face had lost some color and was close enough that if she lifted her hand she could touch his cheeks and nose and lips with her fingers.

It took every ounce of control to keep her hands to herself.

"Not if I get there first to reinforce them. But I'm going to have to leave now."

Without saying anything else, he put her cases in her car.

"Let me help you with the vines—" she blurted.

"Out of the question."

"Why? I'm available. Let's not waste time. All you have to do is give me a job. I want to learn."

His sharp intake of breath spoke volumes about the battle going on inside him.

"Please, Luc. I hadn't planned to stay, but under the circumstances this is one way to repay you for all you've done for me."

"Your generous wine order has more than accomplished that," he bit out.

"Then I take it you don't trust me to do a good job, so I guess that's it. You'd better get going while I check back into the hotel."

She got in her car, feeling on the verge of tears she didn't dare let him see.

He stood at the open window. "Rachel—" His voice grated. "What?"

"Don't think I'm not grateful for your offer."

"Then prove it and let me come with you."

She had no pride left. Her desire to be with him and help him had reduced her to begging for the opportunity.

He muttered something in French she didn't understand. At

the last second when she thought he was going to tell her good-bye she heard,

"Follow me."

Joy surged through her body until she thought she couldn't contain it.

The second she saw his tail-lights go on, she started her car and trailed him. Once they reached the road, Luc took off fast, but she was able to keep up because there wasn't a lot of traffic.

With such an alarming forecast, the locals knew better than to be out in droves.

She'd done it now.

Luc knew she wanted to be with him. Finally Rachel knew he wanted to be with her too. He hadn't been able to let her go yet either.

If he could see into her psyche right now, he would know she never wanted to leave him.

There was a reason for that—she was in love for the first time in her life. So deeply in love she was in pain.

They took a different, faster route to Ribeauville that wound through the foothills past stone houses, castle ruins, even cruci-fixes left over from other centuries.

Once they reached his house on the summit, she pulled in next to his Wagoneer and jumped out to get her suitcase from the back. Luc had already unlocked the door to the house.

"I'll be downstairs," he called to her.

"As soon as I change, I'll join you!"

There was no time to lose. Once inside, she found the bath-room down the hall and discarded her dress for jeans and a T-shirt. After putting on her walking shoes, she raced down the stairs.

Luc had already left for the vineyard through the walkout basement. At a quick glance she noted a bedroom, bathroom and laboratory. Her eyes traveled around the storage room. It was full of tools and vintner equipment, including several boxes of stakes.

She picked up a bundle, reached for a twine holder and headed out the door. In a minute she found him on the west side of the house where the young vines had the longest exposure to light.

Though they were supported by a stake already, they would need more bolstering to survive a violent storm.

She noticed he'd already made progress and was halfway down one of the rows.

"Leave those things at the head of the next row, then come and I'll show you how you can help."

She hurriedly complied.

"We'll make faster time if you tie the stake to the vine after I've driven it into the soil."

She nodded, then got down on her knees to see how much twine to cut, and how exactly to tie the vine.

Watching him work was a revelation to her. No indecision. Every movement was precise, perfect. So quick!

Hers on the other hand were slow and clumsy. But he continually praised her for her efforts. Part of her problem was the knowledge that these were his experimental vines. She didn't want him to lose them.

The next row went a little faster because she'd finally gotten the hang of it. When they came to the end of it, their eyes met.

"I think you've been holding out on me, Rachel. I think you're a vintner's daughter."

Before she could countenance it, he pressed a quick kiss to her lips, then moved on to the next row.

Keep praising me like that and I'm your slave for ever, her heart cried.

A little more than halfway through the plot and she heard the rumblings of thunder.

While she'd been concentrating on her job, the wind had picked up. Strong gusts whipped at her hair. Luckily the ribbon kept most of it out of her face.

"Feel that drop in temperature?" he asked.

"Yes. It was hot again this morning."

"By the time we go inside, I'll have to turn on the heat."

Those words sent certain pictures flashing through her mind. The thought of being alone with him in his own house caused her pulse to pound in her ears.

Afraid Luc could hear it, she worked harder and faster, anxious to finish what they'd started. Helping him like this bonded her to him on a new and deeper level.

Soon the smell of rain filled the air. Bits of leaves and debris began to swirl around them. Another crack of thunder sounded much closer this time, causing her to jump.

She looked up to discover the giant thunderheads she'd noticed earlier were upon them. An eerie darkness had settled in.

Her anxious eyes sought Luc, who was putting in the last set of stakes. Reassured by his presence at her side, she kept on cutting twine and tried not to panic.

Suddenly a bolt of lightning shot out of the blackness. She screamed in fright.

"That was too close!" Luc wheeled around gray-faced and picked her up in his arms. She clung to him as he ran toward the house, carrying her as if she were weightless.

By the time they reached the basement door, hail the size of big marbles beat down on them with enough force to really hurt.

Thunder followed them inside. Even when he'd pulled the door closed, it shook the ground so hard she thought they were having an earthquake.

Terrified, she buried her face in his neck. "I—I've never been in a storm like this before."

He gathered her hard against him. "I should never have let you stay out there this long. Forgive me," he whispered over and over, pressing his lips against her cheek and hair. "I misjudged the speed of the headwinds."

As he spoke lightning illuminated the room.

"There's nothing to forgive," she said, but another tremendous crack of thunder drowned out her words.

She burrowed even closer, needing his strength.

"What kind of a monster am I not to have noticed?" he muttered in self-deprecation. "You risked your life out there for a plot of my damn vines."

His whole body was shuddering now.

The anguish in his voice and eyes seemed to go much deeper than the situation warranted.

"I wasn't aware that's what I was doing," she teased, wanting to comfort him. "Don't forget those damn vines happen to belong to the most celebrated vintner in Alsace."

She would have said anything to take him out of that dark place the storm had triggered. But nothing seemed to be getting through to him.

"Please listen to me. I could have come inside at any time. You're not responsible."

"Of course I am," he ground out. "*Mon Dieu,* Rachel. If anything had happened to you—"

"But it didn't!" she cried, trying with all her power to relieve his pain. "We're safe and sound. But I must say tying vines is dirty work. If you'll put me down, I'll get changed."

He had no concept of how tightly he'd been holding her.

"*Mon Dieu*, you're all right." He half moaned the words. Slowly he relinquished his hold and released her so she could stand on her own.

But he was still worked up. She could tell by the way he raked an unsteady hand through his hair.

"Feel free to take a shower in the guest bathroom. While you do that, I'll clean up and then we'll eat. After all your hard work, you must be starving."

"As soon as I'm ready, I'll join you in the kitchen."

Rachel turned away from him and dashed up the stairs to the bathroom. She'd been in such a hurry before, she hadn't noticed it led to a room that hadn't been furnished yet. She turned on the light but nothing happened. The violence of the storm must have knocked out the power. They would have to eat food that didn't need to be cooked.

Maybe over their meal she could get him to talk about his demons. Something terrible, maybe even tragic, haunted him. If she could ease his suffering a little...

Knowing he was so upset made the pleasure of showering in his brand-new house bittersweet.

After she'd toweled off, she changed back into the same dress she'd been wearing. Once she'd redone her hair with the ribbon and put on fresh lipstick, she hurried past a study with an entertainment center toward the great room she'd seen from the stairs.

On the end wall in the living room he'd built a fire in the stone hearth. A grouping of furniture placed in front of it made the interior incredibly cozy.

The brunt of the storm had moved on. Now there was a steady downpour of rain and the occasional sound of thunder. Rachel wanted to curl up on the couch in his arms and watch the flames that relieved the darkness.

Her gaze darted to the two picture windows framed by red print valences. Both overlooked the steep vineyards below.

She glimpsed a bistro table and two chairs placed in front of the kitchen window. He'd lit a candle so its glow reflected in the glass. The whole atmosphere of the house charmed her.

A few more steps and her heart skipped a beat to see Luc preparing fruit at the counter. He'd changed into a black silk shirt and trousers.

Everything her heart desired was right here... An authentic French country home with an authentic Frenchman so exciting she had trouble believing she wasn't in the middle of some fantastic dream.

His eyes swept over her, taking in every detail of her face and body until it was difficult to breathe. Miraculously the tension that had held him in its grip earlier seemed to have abated, at least for the time being.

"No one would ever guess you'd been out in the dirt slaving to save my *terroir*," he drawled.

"It was worth it even if no vines survived. I have a whole new appreciation for the life of a vintner. While people drink Chartier wines in restaurants all around the world, they don't have a clue what you go through."

His eyes glittered. "Fortunately we don't have storms like this every day, or even every year."

"Nevertheless these cycles of bad weather have to be devastating for those who can't afford to lose even one row of grapes."

"You're right, of course."

"Do you think your other vineyards sustained a lot of damage?"

"I'll know soon enough when my managers have made their assessments."

She moved closer, embarrassed that she was watching him do all the work while they talked.

"What can I do to help?"

His quick smile made her pulse race. *"Grâce à Maman* who brought me a house-warming gift, we have food that doesn't need to be cooked."

Her eyes darted to the table. "But no wine?"

A deep chuckle came out of him that resonated to her bones. *"Hélas, non.* Would you believe the master vintner hasn't had time to stock his own cellar?"

She laughed gently. "This reminds me of an old saying. 'Water, water everywhere, but none to drink.' I'm afraid it's not a very good analogy, but you know what I mean."

"It's a very apt description of the situation," he countered. "Would you like to eat in here, or in front of the fire?"

"Both," she declared. At his surprised look she said, "Let's have the main course in here, and dessert in the other room. I'll supply it." Fire flashed from his eyes.

"It's not what you're thinking," she assured him.

"Chocolate, then?" When he was a boy, he must have driven his mother crazy.

"So you're a chocolate addict."

"I have several vices."

"I see. Well, this is something I think you'll like even better."

"Then let's hurry and eat."

He carried their plates to the table. Rachel sat down on one of the chairs, delighted with the way the seat and back had been woven in strips of white and red.

Everything about his home delighted her. *He* enchanted her.

She watched him devour several individual-sized quiches before she started out eating a sectioned pear. This was the perfect picnic. Their finger food didn't require utensils.

When she bit into her pastry, she noticed his penetrating gaze fixed on her. She took another bite.

"The touch of nutmeg is brilliant."

"You've discovered *Maman's* secret." He sounded pleased.

"This is the best quiche Lorraine I've ever tasted."

"Quiche Alsacienne."

She nodded. "I stand corrected. Tell your mother she could open her own restaurant with food like this. She would put everyone else out of business."

"Coming from you, that's no ordinary compliment."

As soon as they'd finished she got up first and carried their plates to the sink.

"Wait here. I'll be right back."

"Don't take long. I'm an impatient man."

Feverish with anticipation, she flew to the bathroom. After rummaging in her suitcase, she found what she was after wrapped inside her two sweaters.

She put it behind her back and rejoined him in the kitchen where he was cleaning up.

He shot her a mysterious glance. "What are you hiding?"

"It's a surprise."

"If this is a game we're playing, I'll warn you now I don't play fair."

"You think I don't know that? But just this once will you please humor me and close your eyes?"

"That's all I have to do?"

"For now."

Another low chuckle came out of him. "All right. My eyes are closed. For now," he added wryly.

She walked around him and drew two glasses from the cupboard. Then she poured some golden Pinot Gris into each of them.

"I'm going to hand you something."

She pressed a glass into his palm. Their fingers brushed, sending a trail of fire up her arm.

His body stilled. "So the master vintner is now on trial…"

"In a manner of speaking."

His amusement faded as he lifted the glass and breathed in the bouquet.

"You can stop pretending. I already know that *you* know what it is."

Ignoring her comment, he took a swallow and savored it the way she'd done that night at the hotel.

She reached for her own glass and drank from it. Her private salute to the man who'd transformed her into someone she didn't know anymore.

"I detect a new element."

"That's not possible," she challenged. "It's the same Tokay from the bottle you were holding when we met in the hotel."

He opened his eyes and put his empty glass on the counter. To her astonishment he clasped her upper arms.

"I'm never wrong. Let me show you," he whispered in a husky tone. Pulling her close, he covered her wine-glossed lips with his mouth and slowly coaxed them apart as he sought deeper access.

Once again she was overcome by sensations that made her light-headed. She let out a soft gasp of pleasure and wrapped her arms around his neck, the way she'd wanted to do in the pool.

Through the thin material of her dress, he couldn't help but feel her heart cannonading his. It rivaled the thunder that had resounded earlier in the electrified atmosphere.

When he finally lifted his mouth, she groaned.

"Have you discovered it yet?"

"What?" she whispered almost incoherently because he was kissing the throbbing pulse at her throat. "The only thing new I can taste is nutmeg."

His hands roamed over her back, molding her slender curves to his body. "That, and the taste of you," he said on a shallow breath. "There's no recipe for this kind of ambrosia."

Once more he found her mouth in a feverish kiss that went on and on until she lost all sense of time and place. She was on fire for him, matching his desire with her own overpowering need.

She'd had no idea she was capable of this kind of response. But then she'd never been in love before,

"I want you, Rachel," he murmured against her neck. "I want you so much, I'm in agony."

A groan escaped her throat. "I want you, too."

"Do you have any idea how hard it has been to keep my hands off you before now?"

"Yes, because I've suffered the same pain since the first night we met. It's been growing until I haven't been able to think about anything else. Don't ever stop loving me like this, Luc."

"You do know where this is leading."

Right now his hands and mouth were doing the most incredible things to her.

"Yes," she murmured against his lips.

He sucked in his breath. "Something tells me you've never been intimate with a man before. Am I wrong?

"I don't mean this stand-up kind of frenzied kissing.

"I'm talking about the real kind of loving that's a total, unhurried sharing."

Just hearing him say those words caused her legs to go weak. "You're not wrong, Luc. There's never been another man I could be intimate with because—because no man has ever lived up to my ideal except you."

"Is that the truth?" His voice throbbed.

Her eyes blazed into his. "I know I'm an oddity, but I would never lie about something this crucial to my happiness."

He crushed her against him. "Then you don't know what you're asking."

Her heart died a little. "Is my inexperience that distasteful to you?" she cried.

His head reared back. "How could you ask me such a question when you can see I'm totally out of control where you're concerned?"

"Then I don't understand. But it doesn't matter because it's obvious you're haunted by something you're not telling me."

She tore away from his grasp and ran from the kitchen. But she only made it as far as the hallway when she felt arms of steel pull her back against his chest.

"Don't you know I only said that because I'm afraid you'll have regrets?"

She spun around to face him. "If I have any regrets, it's that I didn't keep on going after you caught up with me yesterday afternoon. But it's still not too late to rectify the situation. I'll be leaving as soon as I can get my bags in the car."

"No, Rachel." His voice sounded gravelly. "You're not going

anywhere except to my bed where I plan to love you all weekend long."

The light of desire burned in his eyes, changing his countenance. While her mind tried to comprehend what he'd just said, he picked her up in his arms.

"Give me your luscious mouth," he begged before carrying her down the hall to his room. "It's been a temptation since you called me a lunatic from your car window."

Was that only a few days ago?

Rachel needed no urging to meet his mouth with a hunger she didn't know herself capable of. He'd become her whole world.

CHAPTER SIX

PERHAPS it was the cessation of pounding rain that first brought Rachel out of a deep sleep.

Morning had come to the Vosges. Only a slight drizzle remained to remind her of the storm that had propelled her into Luc's arms.

With renewed hunger, she reached for the man who'd made her feel immortal during the night. Now that she was cognizant of her surroundings, she wanted to know his possession again. Over and over, for the rest of their lives.

After what they'd shared, Rachel was a different woman. She couldn't imagine taking another breath without him being there to bring them both ecstasy.

"Luc." She whispered his name in an aching voice. When she didn't feel his warm body, her eyes opened to discover he wasn't there.

The dim light from outside filled the room. In the place of the indention his head had made on the pillow, she found a note he'd written.

She smoothed the hair out of her eyes and sat up to read it.

Ma belle Rachel—Don't be alarmed. I've had to take care of some business, but I won't be long. Enjoy your beauty sleep while you can.

You are beautiful. Did I tell you?

When I return, I'll come with arms loaded so we can enjoy ourselves without interruption.

Shall it be in my bed, or in front of the fire? Any place with you will suit me perfectly well because you'll be in my arms.

I long to hold you again.

Luc.

Rachel kissed the note, then slid back down under the covers with a voluptuous sigh and pressed it to her chest.

Last night he'd been so tender with her. Intent on giving her pleasure, he'd brought her fulfillment she hadn't known was possible.

Judging by his response, she sensed she'd brought him pleasure too. As the night had worn on, he'd turned to her with greater urgency. They'd both been insatiable. Her face went hot just remembering those hours of rapture.

Finally they'd fallen asleep in each other's arms, exhausted from the intensity of their passion.

She read the note again, euphoric that he was counting the minutes until he could come back to bed where she was waiting for him.

We can enjoy ourselves without interruption. Rachel's toes curled with excitement. The whole weekend to love and be loved by this incredible man.

If anyone could see her now, they'd be shocked by how breathless she was, waiting to experience the miracle of his lovemaking all over again.

He'd told her to catch up on her beauty sleep, but that would be impossible. She was wide awake, embarrassingly eager for his return.

She checked her watch. It was eight-twenty. Rachel had no idea when he'd left, but she imagined it would be a while before she heard his car pull in.

Deciding to fix herself some fruit and coffee, she slid out of the bed with the intention of taking a shower and washing her hair first. The room was cold.

But the sight of her clothes flung haphazardly on the floor brought another wave of heat to her cheeks, warming her clear through. She paused long enough to gather them up and put them on a chair before going into the bathroom.

She flicked on the light, but nothing happened. Still no power. Forget hot coffee.

Her eyes darted to his yellow toweling robe. It hung from a hook on the door. She buried her face in the fabric where she could smell the scent of the soap he used.

After her shower, she put it on, loving the feel of something he wore all the time wrapped around her body.

She cinched in the belt at the waist, then reached for a striped towel and dried her hair as best she could.

Later she would blow-dry it, but right now she was ravenous and left the bathroom for the kitchen. Maybe there was another quiche left to go with one of those delicious pears.

The first thing she saw sitting on the counter was her bottle of wine, a wineglass and a half quiche lying on a plate. He'd left another note.

A loaf of bread, a jug of wine and thou...
Forgive me for stealing half the loaf. As you've found out, I'm a man with several appetites. You're at the top of my list.
Luc.

She smiled and trembled at the same time in anticipation of his arrival. How she loved him!

This was better than breakfast in bed. This was Luc, so wonderful, so unique in every way. No man compared to him.

Delighted by the love feast he'd placed before her, she poured herself a little wine. It wasn't just any wine.

This came from the Tokay grapes grown in his vineyard, nurtured with all the love and concern of a parent for his child.

Between bites of quiche, she took swallows of the handcrafted elixir created by a master. As its warmth spread through her body, she could imagine it was Luc's hands caressing her, making her aware of her womanhood in a way only he could do. There was no heat like it.

She felt sorry for every woman who'd never been loved by a man like him.

Just thinking about him made her heart thud wildly. That was his effect on her and always would be.

Always.

She had plans for them.

Dreams...

In the midst of her reverie, she thought she heard footsteps coming from the foyer. She spun around and called out Luc's name in a voice of pure joy.

"*Non*. It is not Luc," said the slim older woman who'd entered the kitchen carrying a covered basket. She had to be five feet seven, Rachel's height.

She didn't know who was more surprised as the two appraised each other for what seemed like minutes. The other woman had spoken English in the same heavy French accent as Luc.

Her brown hair was cut short and stylishly. She wore a small silver crucifix around her neck. The top of her outfit reminded Rachel of an artist's smock. It was chic and suited her.

"I'm his mother, Madame Chartier."

Rachel reeled.

His mother?

With all the confidence of a parent who felt as at home in her son's house as her own, she put the basket on the counter near the wine bottle and plate.

Rachel didn't know if his mother had been able to read the contents of the note before she'd turned to her. "And you are..."

The more Rachel studied her, the more she could see the resemblance in the arched eyebrows and those dark brown eyes staring at her with that same startling penetration.

But instead of intense male admiration, Madame Chartier's eyes gave off a hostility that was barely veiled.

"I'm Rachel Valentine, *madame*." She swallowed hard. "It's very nice to meet you."

The tension was palpable.

"You're the buyer from the UK."

"That's right."

His mother's attractive features hardened. "You've come to the Wine Route of Alsace. There are over a hundred little villages with hotels, yet you couldn't find a room in one of them while you did business here?"

Her disapproving gaze examined Rachel from her damp, disheveled hair to her bare feet.

"I ended up here because of the storm."

"I see."

"Luc said it was too dangerous to go anywhere."

"Was that before or after you sent our office your wine order?"

The question hung out there like a live wire.

"After," she answered honestly. "We were afraid the vines in the vineyard here would be destroyed, so I came with him to help him tie them to some more stakes."

His mother's wrists were crossed over her flat stomach.

"How clever of you to ingratiate yourself in a way my son couldn't possibly have refused."

"Look, Madame Chartier, I—"

"No explanation is necessary," she cut Rachel off. "The situation speaks for itself. How soon do you expect my son?"

"I—I don't know." Her voice faltered. "He said he had business. I would imagine he's out surveying any damage to his other vineyards."

"You would be wrong in that assumption, *mademoiselle*. His managers would have already phoned him if there'd been anything serious to report. The business he has every morning is at the hospital in St Hippolyte."

Rachel frowned. Was he on the board? With his prominence, he was probably involved with several civic institutions.

His mother put her hands in the pockets of her sage-colored top. "I can see he's told you nothing."

Rachel took a fortifying breath. "We haven't known each other long."

"Long enough apparently."

Those shrewd dark eyes wandered over the robe Rachel was wearing.

"His sister bought that last year for his thirty-fourth birthday. She'd be surprised to see anyone else wearing it."

"I'm sorry you had to see me in it," Rachel apologized. "I realize it has come as a shock to find me here."

"A bigger shock than you can imagine."

"Naturally you wouldn't have known about me. I only came to Alsace on Monday," Rachel explained in the hope of making this easier on both of them.

"So I understand from Giles." Her eyes narrowed. "How soon do you intend to return to England?"

"I'm not sure," she murmured. It was up to Luc. But if his mother had anything to say about it, Rachel would be out the door and gone from the area within five minutes.

A strange sound came from the other woman. "My son has been his own man for many years. Until now, he has made wise decisions."

Rachel took the bait. She couldn't help it. "Is it me particularly you have a problem with?"

She had to wait a long time for an answer.

"I don't know enough to like or dislike you, *mademoiselle*. But you are a very beautiful woman. My son would have to be blind not to be attracted."

Rachel shook her head in misery and exasperation. "I still don't understand."

"How could you if he didn't tell you?"

Her heart hammered in alarm. "Tell me what? Please, I want to know."

His mother gazed at her speculatively, as if pondering whether to say anything or not.

"He has a wife."

"Luc told me he was divorced." Rachel refused to believe he'd lied to her. That wasn't the Luc she knew.

"Not in the eyes of the church. Two days after the proceeding became final, the car accident happened because Paulette was beside herself at the time and realized the divorce was a mistake.

"God willing, one day soon she'll wake up from her coma.

At that moment they'll remarry because he's never stopped loving her, nor she him."

Rachel groaned.

His mother looked all around the room. "He built this house for her. It's a gift to represent a new beginning."

The world tilted for a moment.

"How long has she been in that state?"

"Three years."

Three?

"He hasn't missed a day at her bedside. Nor has he stopped willing her to wake up and love him again. Her family is fighting him in court to get the machines turned off. He won't hear of it, and is using his financial resources to make certain that doesn't happen."

A knot of pain twisted Rachel's insides.

"Not even you could keep him away from her this morning. I'm not telling you this to be hateful. You've heard the expression, 'Sometimes we have to be cruel to be kind.' I'm simply trying to save you future grief.

"What you decide to do from here on out is your affair. *Adieu, mademoiselle.*"

Adieu meant goodbye for ever.

Numb from shock, Rachel could only stand there helplessly as she watched his mother leave the kitchen and disappear out the front door.

"If something seems too good to be true, it always is."

That was what Rachel's embittered mother had used to say in those years following the divorce.

A coldness began to seep into her body. The kind where you didn't think you could ever be warm again.

There was no doubt in her mind the older woman had told her the truth. Madame Chartier had no reason to lie.

It would be easy enough to call the hospital and receive verification that Luc's ex-wife was a patient.

Divorce didn't mean you stopped loving a person. If anyone understood that, Rachel did.

Though her father had married four times, he'd claimed Rachel's mother had been the great love of his life.

Rachel knew it was true. The marriage before he'd met her mother had been a mistake.

After her parents' divorce, his other marriages hadn't been able to fill up the empty spaces in his life.

Her father was an emotional mess. But she had to admit she saw a look come into his eyes whenever he talked about her mother.

If she were still alive, Rachel was positive he'd try to get her to marry him again.

Even though he failed as a husband and father in so many ways, the emotion for her mother would always be there, no matter what.

The emotion Luc felt for his ex-wife would always be there. No matter what.

Rachel had known he was a rare man. To hear he'd spent the last three years devoted to her made him exceptional.

It also made a future with him impossible. He had demons all right, ones she couldn't fight.

Rachel wasn't like her father's last two wives, wanting any crumbs he threw them. She would have to be the only woman in Luc's heart, but she wasn't. She never would be.

His great love Paulette was lying in a hospital bed, capable of waking up at any time.

Miracles like that *did* happen. That was what Luc was praying for.

By being brutally honest, Madame Chartier had done Rachel the greatest favor of her life.

She was an intruder and needed to be gone from this house now!

Five minutes later she'd dressed and loaded her bags in the car. Ten minutes later her travel agent had arranged a flight to London from Basel, Switzerland.

En route across the border Rachel phoned Monsieur Bulot in Châlons, and placed a wine order that would satisfy him and her father.

Everyone would be satisfied…except for one person.

The woman who'd awakened this morning full of sublime joy…had just died.

* * *

Luc paid for his groceries and went out to the Wagoneer. As he was putting the bags in the back seat his cell phone went off.

He glanced at the caller ID and clicked on. "*Bonjour*, Paul."

"*Bonjour*. I'm phoning to tell you I cancelled the court date for Monday per your instructions."

"Good. Now that Yves and I have made our peace, I can breathe more easily."

"I'm sure it was a difficult decision for you, but, speaking as your friend as well as your attorney, I think you've done the right thing."

"So do I. Yves insists Paulette wants out of her bondage. Their family has agreed to give me until the end of the summer."

"Why then? I'm curious."

"I guess it has been the vintner in me. You know—the hope of a successful harvest in the fall."

"You're still so young, Luc. There are many successful fall harvests in your future, new vintages, if you follow my meaning."

Luc had aleady found that out during those rapturous hours of the night.

"So Giselle has continually reminded me. Thank you, Paul."

"You're welcome. Let's go to lunch next week."

"I'll call you."

He hung up and headed for the house. Thanks to Rachel, his plot of experimental vines had survived the storm. After inspecting his vineyard earlier this morning, he'd only counted five plants that were lost.

His heart did a fierce kick just contemplating being alone with her for the rest of the weekend. The only reason he'd left her this long was to drive to Thann for a certain artifact he needed to carry out a plan he had in mind.

But his excitement waned when he came in sight of his house and couldn't see her rental car.

He would have known if he'd seen her on the road. She must have gone to the nearest village for something she needed. He parked the car and took everything in the house, anxious to read her note.

It wasn't until he put his things on the kitchen counter that he noticed the large, familiar basket placed next to the empty plate and wine.

There was only one note. The same one he'd left for Rachel...

Bile rose in his throat imagining the scenario. "Holy mother of God."

During his frantic trip to St Hippolyte he phoned Rachel's cell, but she'd turned it off.

He rang Georges at the car rental agency, but the other man was off for the weekend. No one knew anything about Ms Valentine's itinerary, not since a car had been provided for her on Thursday.

On automatic pilot now, he drove to his mother's house. When he couldn't find her inside, he raced around the back. She was in the garden surveying the damage to the flowers from the storm.

The way she eyed him let him know she'd been waiting for him.

"You'd better take time to catch your breath before you try to speak, *mon fils*."

It had been twenty-five years at least since his mother had tried to shrivel him with her disappoval.

"All I want to know is how much you told her."

Her brows arched. "Quite a bit—since you failed to tell her anything."

His eyes closed tightly for a moment. "Why, *Maman?*"

"If she'd been a woman who wouldn't think twice about sleeping with any available man, I would have told her I was the cleaning woman, and then I would have left."

Luc rubbed his hand over his face.

"But I realized at once she wasn't like that. Not at all. I sensed a vulnerability about her...and a sweetness you don't often see. Considering the circumstances, I must admit I've never met anyone with more poise."

His mother gave him a fierce look. "She's a lovely woman, Luc. Too lovely inside and out to have lied to her the way you did."

"There were no lies between us," he bit out heatedly.

"*Non?* Did Paulette's name ever pass your lips?"

"Rachel knew I was divorced. This morning I had plans to tell her everything."

"You're too late." She shook her head. "A woman like that gives her heart with her body. Before she even saw me, she thought it was you.

"If you could have heard the joy in her voice, or have seen the stars in her eyes… How could you do it, Luc?"

Anger ripped through him. "I'm sorry, *Maman*, but this is none of your business."

"It became my business because you didn't tell her the whole truth, and you kept your interest in her a secret from me. Secrets have a way of coming out.

"I had no idea that car belonged to her. I thought it might have been one of the workmen's who'd come to finish up something on your house.

"It wasn't until I left that I noticed it was a rental car."

"By then it was too late and the damage had been done," he finished in a savage tone.

"No, Luc. You did the damage all by yourself when you brought her to your house. If she has left the area, then she's gone way up in my estimation. A real woman doesn't cling to a man whose heart is somewhere else."

Anger consumed him. "You don't know what's in my heart, *Maman*."

"I know it wasn't your heart that made love to Mademoiselle Valentine. Let's be honest about that.

"But I saw into hers when I told her you'd been at Paulette's bedside three years waiting for her to wake up."

Luc could only imagine it. Every word from his mother tore his gut up a little more. A whole new world of agony had dawned.

He gritted his teeth. "Since this is a day for the telling of secrets, you should know I've talked with Yves. I'm no longer fighting his family. The lawyers have been notified. There'll be no court case.

"If Paulette hasn't come out of her coma by the end of August, then that's it."

"I don't believe it," his mother whispered. "It's because of that w—"

"Don't, *Maman!*" he silenced her. "Don't go there. You don't know everything."

"How dare you say that to me?"

It hurt him to be at odds with her, but certain things needed to be said. Now was the moment.

"You've been grieving since *Papa* died. It has colored your thinking. For a long time it has colored mine. But no longer."

"Hi, Max."

His brown head lifted. "Rachel—when did you get back?"

"Late last night."

Her flight from Basel had been delayed by bad weather. More rain had greeted her at Heathrow. But she decided it was a blessing. People would attribute the moisture bathing her face to the elements.

"I brought you a present."

She pulled a bottle of Chartier Riesling from her tote bag and placed it on the desk where he was going over the accounts.

He sat back with a grin to examine the label. "Now *this* is what I call a present! You should go to France every month."

No. Never again.

"I'm afraid those days are over for me."

His bright blue eyes squinted up at her. "What do you mean?"

"I'm changing careers."

"Over Dad's dead body."

Better his than mine. "Has he come in yet?"

"No. It's Sunday. He's probably still doing laps in the pool." Max scrutinized her for a long moment.

"What's going on? For someone lucky enough to be in France for the last two weeks, you look terrible."

"I'm worried about Grandfather."

"We all are, but something else has turned you inside out."

She averted her eyes. "This trip I realized I've learned all that's necessary about wine. I'm ready to go into restaurant management, like you."

He scoffed. "Tell me another story. You don't walk in here and drop a bomb like that expecting to get away with it.

"For one thing, Bella Lucia already has too many managers all in one family."

"Agreed. I'm planning to hire on with another kind of restaurant altogether and work my way up."

"That's bull."

"Just stand back and watch me."

After a brief silence, "Okay. It's obvious something *bad* has happened to you. I can handle it if you don't want to tell me about it. Just don't let Dad get wind of your new plans. He'll view it as high treason."

No, Max. High treason involves murdering the soul. That honor has gone to a certain unforgettable Frenchman.

His gaze darted to her purse. "Your cell phone's ringing."

Yes, she knew. It had been ringing on the hour for the last twenty-four.

"Aren't you at least going to see who it is?"

She smoothed a lock of hair away from her temple. "No one knows I'm back yet, so it can wait. Has Emma come in? I have a present for her too."

He nodded. "In the dining room going over tonight's menu with the *sous-chef* and rest of the kitchen staff."

"Thanks, brother dear." Sharing the same difficult father with Max and Emma made Rachel and her half-siblings close. There was strength in unity. "See you tomorrow when I'm officially back."

"Rachel?"

She paused in the doorway of the office.

"I'm here if you need to unload."

There was no way she could tell him about the nightmarish scene in Luc's kitchen. Madame Chartier's revelations had crushed her world to grist.

"I love you for saying that. By the way, consider that I've just given you my notice. If you don't find a new wine buyer for Bella Lucia in the next few weeks I'm sorry, but I'll be gone."

Without saying anything else she moved through the back hallway to the dining area of the restaurant.

It was classic Georgian on the outside, the recently refurbished interior reflecting neutral walls and a chic, understated sophistication.

Though Rachel liked it well enough, she agreed with her

grandfather who'd preferred the original Italian décor. But he was a business genius and knew not to stand in the way of progress.

Her grandfather.

She needed him. Now more than ever.

As soon as she'd talked to Emma, she would go straight over to his house in St John's Wood and spend the rest of the day with him.

She walked around the linen-covered tables toward the group of seven seated near the kitchen doors. Rachel gave a small wave to Emma, whose honey-blond head had turned in her direction.

Emma must have said something to the others. They all called out greetings and welcomed her back before leaving her and Emma alone.

Rachel rushed forward and hugged her diminutive half sister. "How's Grandfather?" she asked after they'd let go of each other.

"Not good. I've been sleeping in the ante-room for the last couple of nights."

"Now that I'm back, we'll take turns. Since I'm going over there in a few minutes, I'll plan to sleep there tonight."

"I'm glad you're home," Emma admitted in a tremulous voice. "He's been waiting for you to get back. It's going to cheer him up so much to see you."

Tears welled in Rachel's eyes. "What does Dr Lloyd say?"

"His oxygen level is still too low, and the pain on his right side is worse. There's also been some new swelling in his lower legs where the clots first started."

"Oh, Emma—I can't bear it. Don't you think he needs to be in the hospital?"

By now Emma's pale blue eyes were swimming in liquid. "He refuses to go. You know how he is. He talked the doctor and Uncle John into arranging for round-the-clock nursing care. They're using the bedrooms on the third floor."

"What about the house staff?"

"Grandfather asked Dad to be in charge and make certain they get paid on time."

The two of them stared knowingly at each other. "The tension between them must be awful."

Emma nodded. She looked distressed and tired. As for Rachel...

"I brought you a couple of things." She reached in her bag and put another bottle of Riesling on the table.

"Ooh," Emma said, wiping her eyes. "The real thing "

"Yes. I brought you something else too." She handed her the cookbook.

Emma opened the cover. "An eighteen ninety-two first edition!" she exclaimed.

Rachel smiled to hear the delight in her voice. "I've read through it, and some of those recipes sound marvelous."

"I'm sure they are! Thank you, Rachel. You'll have to help me translate." They hugged once more. "I can't wait to try some of them out. That sauerkraut recipe was fantastic!"

"I thought it was. It'll be even better with this Riesling."

Emma put the bottle in the crook of her arm. "All I have to do is get Dad's approval. You know how he is about changes in the menu."

"I don't think you'll have any problems after he samples my gifts for him. I was hoping he'd be here, but since he isn't, I'm going to Grandfather's right now."

"Not so fast," their father interjected.

"Hi, Dad."

"Morning, Emma."

Rachel turned to see their tall, good-looking father walk toward them dressed in a royal blue sport shirt and beige trousers.

Though he was in his sixties, he still looked fit and had a good head of hair. The gray flecks mixed among the black gave him a distinguished appearance.

"So you're back."

She nodded. "Late last night."

His gaze flicked to Emma. "Have you gone over tonight's menu yet?"

"It's already done. I'll be in the kitchen if you need me. See you later."

After she left, Rachel kissed his cheek. "It's good to see you. How's Titan?"

"Doing better. How was your visit with Jacques Bulot?"

She took a quick extra breath. "We ended up doing business over the phone."

His black eyes snapped in irritation. "How come?"

She'd prepared herself for that question.

"I got so worried about Grandfather, I decided to cut my trip short. But it's all right. I placed a big order for champagne. When I told him about Grandfather, he completely understood and sent his personal regards."

He pursed his lips. "Father's on his last legs."

It was one thing to think it, but another to hear it expressed so baldly.

"I hope and pray not." She reached in her bag for his gifts. "These are for you."

She put his favorite whiskey and a bottle of the grand cru label Pinot Gris on the table.

"Oh, and this—" She felt deeper for the box of cigars he liked.

"You're a regular Mary Poppins." With that remark a little of his humor had returned. If she could just keep him that way.

He went straight for the Tokay and uncorked it. "*This* is what kept you in Alsace?" he demanded.

If her father only knew… But he was one person she'd never been able to confide in. He didn't care enough about anyone else's problems to show more than a surface concern. He wasn't like her grandfather.

"Try it and you'll understand why."

There was a clean wineglass handy. He reached for it and poured himself a generous amount.

Without bothering to savour it, he drank it in several swallows the way he did his whiskey.

The aftertaste was part of what made it so wonderful. She waited for him to say something.

"What's that flavor?"

"Which one?"

He eyed her for a minute. "You're the expert. You're supposed to tell me."

No. There was only one expert. The mere thought of him brought raw, stabbing pain.

"I'm going to let you think about it for a while." She reached for her tote bag and started walking toward the entrance to the restaurant.

"Rachel?"

"Yes, Dad?" she called over her shoulder.

"Whatever it is, it's damn good."

"I'm glad you approve since I've ordered sixty cases for starters. And that's only their Tokay. Wait till you taste their Riesling!"

"How much is this costing us?"

"A lot, but I can guarantee Chartier white wines are going to bring in repeat customers until we have to turn them away in droves. This trip I found out French bread isn't France's greatest contribution to the world after all. Alsace is."

She'd learned something else, too. *I'm the world's greatest fool. That makes me your daughter, Daddy.*

CHAPTER SEVEN

"PHILIPPE?"

"*Bonjour,* Luc."

"I hate bothering you on Sunday, but this is important. I have to go out of town as soon as I've been to the hospital."

His flight from Colmar to London would be leaving in two hours. That only gave him a few minutes to check on Paulette.

"Giles is in charge until I get back. If there's an emergency he can't deal with, he'll call me. In the meantime, if anyone phones asking for me, just take their number and I'll get back to them when I return."

"*Très bien. A toute à l'heure.*"

No matter how great Philippe's curiosity might be, he was the soul of discretion who never pried or questioned Luc's directives. That made him worth his weight in gold.

As Luc climbed out of the Maserati he noticed Yves' green car in the emergency parking area.

Fearing something had happened to him or one of his family—the children, maybe—he rushed inside the hospital. The triage nurse checked the board. No Brouet had been admitted.

That meant something had to be wrong with Paulette— Why hadn't the hospital phoned *him?*

A surge of adrenaline sent him bounding up the stairs to her floor. Yves was standing at the nursing station. The second he saw Luc, he came running and grabbed his shoulders, sounding out of breath.

"I was just telling the staff to phone you and the parents."

"What's happened?"

"Paulette's eyes opened while I was holding her hand. Maybe you were right and she's starting to wake up!"

Luc's heart slammed against his chest cavity, bringing him out of the shock Yves' words had just given him.

"They've sent for the doctor, but the resident is in with her now," Yves explained as they both rushed toward her room.

For so long Luc had been waiting for this moment. But when he approached her bed and saw her fixed brown stare that showed no recognition or eye movement, his body went cold.

Those weren't her eyes. There was no spark, no animation. Her body still lay there lifeless while the nurse was taking her vital signs.

Luc felt as if someone had just slammed their foot in his chest. He didn't want this picture of her to stay in his mind. But if it meant she was coming out of the coma...

"What's going on with her?"

The resident turned to them. "That's for Dr Soulier to determine after he studies the printout. My advice is to keep her stimulated until he gets here."

Yves took his place on the other side of her bed and lifted her hand. Luc reached for her other hand, They took turns talking to her, but all Luc saw in her eyes was a vacuum. The moment was surreal.

In a few minutes he heard people out in the hall. A woman's high-pitched voice was chattering excitedly.

Soon three people came in the room. Paulette's parents and the doctor.

Luc moved to the side so his mother-in-law could take his place.

"Oh, my darling Paulette. My darling girl. It's your *maman*. Can you see me now? Can you hear me?"

All a mother's love was in her voice. By now Paulette's father was standing next to Yves, holding his daughter's hand.

Luc's throat swelled with emotion because they, too, wanted so much more from her than that glassy-eyed stare. They wanted her back, fully alive and whole.

"Does this mean she's waking up?" Madame Brouet cried with tears running down her face.

The doctor's solemn gaze took in all of them. "I see no brain-wave activity. There's been no verbal or motor response. But she has opened her eyes.

"Whether because of pain, or because Yves was speaking to her, or because she did it on her own, we don't know yet. We'll have to wait and see if there's more response.

"In the meantime I'll instruct the staff to keep her eyes moistened. I have rounds to make, then I'll check on her again."

After he left the room, Paulette's mother turned to Luc. She grabbed his forearms. "Forgive me for fighting you all this time. Thank you, *mon fils*, for not giving up!" she cried before hugging him with surprising strength.

She hadn't called him her son for so long. Luc's arms closed around her. She was a little thing like Paulette.

How strange that at the moment Paulette's mother was starting to believe in miracles, he had the presentiment there wouldn't be one in Paulette's case.

When he'd been a boy about seven or eight, he'd found an injured bird in the vineyard after a storm. He'd picked it up and run to his father who had been able to fix anything.

But his parent had just shaken his head and said, "He's gone."

"But his eyes are open, *Papa*."

"Sometimes that's the way it is."

"We'll all stay here for the rest of the night and pray for another sign," Paulette's father announced, jerking Luc back to the present.

There'd be no flight to London this evening.

Rachel held the digital camera screen in front of her grandfather's eyes so he could look at Solange and Giles.

"I see a strong resemblance to Louis."

"When you get better, you can tell her that in person." She put the camera on the bedstand. "Do you want one of the truffles I brought you from Switzerland?'

"Maybe lat—" He broke off, coughing.

Rachel was in shock to see that, in two weeks, he'd gone downhill.

"What's the matter, my sweet girl? You left for France with a light in your eyes. Now it's gone." His coughing shook the bed. "I detect all the signs of a man. I've wondered when it was finally going to happen."

She bowed her head to hide her anguish, but it was too late. Her grandfather knew her better than anyone. His compassion found that secret place inside her where all her pain was locked up. Suddenly she was convulsed.

"As soon as you're able, tell me what he did to bring you so much pain."

She lay her head on his arm. Throughout his episodes of coughing and the sobs that shook her body, she unburdened her soul to him. When she'd finished, he patted her head.

"This could take some time to sort out."

Rachel rose up. She wiped the tears off her chin. "It's over, Grandfather."

"Don't be so sure. Life is full of surprises when we least expect them. In the meantime I have an idea."

"What is it?"

"When Dr Lloyd tells me I'm well enough to travel, let's get on a plane and go visit Rebecca. It'll be just the three of us. I've missed her and know you have, too.

"When you were little, you were inseparable and told each other everything. You two need each other."

Once again Rachel was overcome by emotions buried deep in her heart. She squeezed his hand because she couldn't talk.

Rachel rested her head against his shoulder again, lost in thought, and it was a few minutes before she realized he'd fallen asleep. That was what he needed.

She tiptoed into the adjoining room where she planned to stay. It had twin beds.

When Rachel had come to the mansion, she'd taken her suitcase and laptop in there before going in to her grandfather.

Walking over to the dresser, she pulled the cell phone out of her purse. At a glance she saw that every recorded message came from Luc's caller ID.

He could phone all he wanted, but there was nothing to say.

In anguish, she rang the nurse upstairs and told her she should come down now.

Then Rachel phoned information for the number of Rebecca's best friend. Stephanie Ellison lived in London and would be able to give her Rebecca's cell-phone number.

Now that Rebecca was in Wyoming, Rachel didn't have the faintest idea where to reach her.

After a short conversation with Stephanie, who was happy to give it to her, Rachel placed the call.

It was noon in London, which meant five o'clock in the morning in Wyoming.

After that fiasco phone call with Rebecca almost a week ago, she didn't believe her sister would ever need her or want to talk to her again.

But for once Rachel didn't feel hesitant about what to say. This was an emergency.

The phone rang three times before a man answered. He put Rebecca on the line straight away.

"Rebecca? Stephanie helped me locate you. It's Grandfather William. I—I'm afraid he's dying."

Her sister gasped in pain. Rachel felt it from thousands of miles away.

"He wants us to fly to New York so the three of us can be together, but that isn't possible. So I'm begging you to get on the next plane.

"Though Dr Lloyd isn't saying much, something tells me Grandfather's time is coming close. If he were to pass away this next week, and you weren't here…"

Rachel couldn't speak for a minute. "All I'm saying is, I wouldn't want you to suffer the way I did when Mother died so unexpectedly. Even though I was on my way to be with her, I wasn't able to get there in time. It killed me." Her voice shook.

"I suppose Grandfather could linger for a while longer, but he talked about you tonight. He wants to see you, Rebecca. So come as fast as you can."

While she waited for her answer, a man's voice came on the line.

"Rachel, this is Mitch Tucker. I'll make sure your sister gets on a plane."

She blinked. "Thank you, Mr Tucker. Our family needs her."
Whoever he was, Rachel was grateful.

She clicked off before collapsing on the bed. Once more sobs
shook her body to think her grandfather wasn't long for this earth.

There'd been too many losses over the years. Her parents' divorce, the deaths of her mother and grandmother. Too much separation from her sister and Crawford grandparents, too many
missed opportunities.

And since her trip to France, now this new pain had come into
her life. The death of a dream.

A dream too good to be true. In real life Luc continued to
mourn for his ex-wife who hovered between life and death.

Madame Chartier had spoken the truth. When you loved
someone as much as Luc loved Paulette, a decree of divorce
meant nothing.

Three years at her bedside when he didn't have to be…

"Good evening, sir. Welcome to the Bella Lucia. How many are
in your party?"

Luc's eyes took in everything at a glance. From the understated elegance of the foyer you could either go left to the dining
room, or right to the bar.

"I'm not here to dine. I have an appointment with your wine
buyer, Ms Valentine. I missed my flight from France yesterday,
so we made arrangements for tonight."

"I see. What's your name and I'll let her know you're here?"

"That won't be necessary. She told me to walk on back to her
office when I arrived. Thank you."

Luc strode down the hall as if he knew exactly where to go.
At this point he didn't care how many lies he had to tell in order
to speak to her.

After arriving at Heathrow, he'd gone straight to her flat, but
she hadn't answered the door. That left him with no choice but
to corner her here where she couldn't run from him.

Judging by the crowd, Bella Lucia did a flourishing business.
When he didn't see her behind the bar, he kept on going. There
were several doors, none with signs.

He opened the first one, having no idea what he'd find. It was an office with no personal items to tell him if it belonged to a man or a woman. But just as he turned to leave he noticed a bottle of Chartier Riesling on top of a file cabinet.

Interesting, since he happened to know Tokay was her favorite.

Behind the next door he found what he was looking for. Not only was there a stack of wine menus on the shelf, he spied an assortment of small framed pictures on the desk.

He was drawn to the one of a young Rachel and her twin sister. They were probably eleven or twelve, mounted on horseback and showing the proper carriage of expert equestrians.

No doubt the other pictures represented her parents and extended family.

Luc figured she was bound to come in her office before she went home. While he waited, he reached for one of the menus to examine. She'd put a nice list together of probably three hundred wines.

Naturally it was too soon for Chartier et Fils to have been added yet. It was only Monday evening. Two days since her flight from his house above Ribeauville.

As he was putting the menu back he heard voices outside the door, then it opened.

Rachel's fragrance preceded her into the office. A faint sweet scent of roses that had clung to his bathrobe and the pillows on his bed.

Luc was behind the door so she didn't immediately see him. "Rachel?"

She gasped before spinning around. The force caused the material of her filmy lavender dress to swish around her legs.

But the lovely face before him had gone white. Her eyes were a nondescript gray, not the dreamy blue he remembered.

She looked ill. The change in her devastated him.

He hardly recognized her from the last time he'd seen her with her dark glossy hair fanned across the pillow, the lashes of her closed lids brushing against cheeks turned rosy by their lovemaking.

"You've wasted your time by coming here," she stated in a dull voice.

Exhibiting a composure that left him incredulous, she walked behind her desk and unlocked a drawer to pull out her purse.

He moved closer. "We have to talk, Rachel. My mother told me what happened. Unfortunately she only sees and understands things from her perspective as a widow who hasn't come to terms with my father's death yet.

"You should have known that ignoring my phone calls wouldn't keep me away."

She eyed him without as much as a flicker of her lashes. He could scarcely credit her display of sang-froid.

"When I didn't answer one of them, you should have known to leave well enough alone."

He grimaced. "After what we shared, you should know I can't and won't accept that."

"I agree we enjoyed a very special night together. Now it's over, and I have to go."

"It was much more than that and you know it," he bit out. "Paulette and I haven't been husband and wife for three years, Rachel."

"As your mother said, a piece of paper ending a marriage doesn't necessarily make it so. Your devotion to Paulette leaves me in awe."

She started for the door.

"Rachel—" he ground out.

"Don't you get it?" Her cheeks flamed. "I wish I hadn't been the woman you used in a moment of weakness. But that's my fault for not listening to you when you warned me I might have regrets.

"As I told you during the storm, I could have gone inside at any time. I could have gotten in my car and left your house at any time after that. But I didn't. All my fault. And now, just as you thought, I have regrets. Besides not saving myself for marriage, I dishonored the woman you married for better for worse, in sickness and in health. Please stand aside."

He remained in place. "You're not leaving until I tell you everything I should have told you after I asked you to stay for the weekend.

"I want to explain so you'll understand what's been going on inside me."

"Inside *you*?" Her head reared back. "You have no conception of what you've done to me!"

"You're wrong," he whispered in pain.

She shook her head. "Why couldn't you have told me while we were swimming? Or during dinner at the Petit Vosges?"

Luc groaned to see the anguish on her beautiful face.

"I was tormented, Rachel. I didn't want you to leave Alsace, but I knew I couldn't make any promises to you because Paulette is still alive. I'm still committed to being there for her."

Her eyes were wild with pain. "So you took your pleasure behind everyone's back!"

Her salvo found its mark. "I wish to God I'd handled things differently."

"So do I!" He felt her body trembling. "When you first told me you were divorced, what you should have said was, 'My wife's lying in a coma.'

"*That* would have done it for me because it would only have been the truth! I would have placed my order with Giles the next day and been long gone. Now please move away from the door."

His chest tightened. "Not until you hear me out."

"This conversation comes a lifetime too late!" Her features looked like chiseled marble.

"Nevertheless I'm not going anywhere. You deserve to hear the truth from me, not my mother's version."

Pain and sorrow glinted in her eyes, shaking him to the core before she eventually sank down in the chair in defeat.

"I want you to know everything from the very beginning.

"I was twenty-seven when I married Paulette Brouet. She was twenty-two, the little sister of my best friend Yves.

"We weren't childhood sweethearts. I had several meaningful relationships with women before I began to notice her in a different light. Somewhere along the way I fell in love and we got married.

"She wanted children right away, but it took three years for her to conceive our son."

He heard a gasp of shock before Rachel's head came up.

"You mean my mother didn't tell you?"

"No," she whispered.

He leaned against the door. "At Paulette's six-months check-up, the doctor couldn't find a heartbeat."

A compassionate cry escaped Rachel's throat despite her anger at him.

"Miscarriages happen. Yves' wife had one. My mother had two. I was devastated, but the doctor assured us she could have another baby.

"Paulette was inconsolable; I knew it was natural for her to feel that way. Her hormones had put her in a severe depression.

"I did everything I could to bring her out of it. A few months later I took her on a cruise, hoping to get her pregnant again. To my shock, she asked me not to touch her."

Rachel's hands went to the sides of her chair, as if bracing herself.

"I realized she was still grieving for our unborn child. So I left her alone, hoping time would heal the worst of her pain.

"Six months to the day the baby died, she said she wanted a divorce.

"I consulted a psychiatrist. He said she had an irrational fear of getting pregnant again and then losing it. If she would let him, he could help her. But she had become so emotionally disturbed, she wouldn't hear of it and moved home with her family."

Rachel jumped up from the chair. "I don't think I want to hear any more."

"I'm almost through. At first I fought our separation, but Yves talked me into going along with it. He was convinced that in time she'd get over the worst of the loss and want to get back with me.

"I wanted to believe it, so I agreed. To make things easier all the way around, I gave her the house I'd bought for us, and I moved in with my family.

"Two days after our divorce was final, she was involved in a car accident. When I was told she was lying unconscious in the hospital, a new nightmare began."

Rachel refused to look at him. "I can't imagine how you've managed to make it through life this long.

"Go back to her bedside, Luc. I'm going to my grandfather's."

He put a hand on her arm. "Is he worse?"

Her lower lip trembled, the first sign to let him know she was barely holding on.

"This morning Dr Lloyd admitted he's dying." There was a brief pause. "Unlike Paulette who could possibly wake up from her coma, there's no such hope for Grandfather."

"I'm sorry, Rachel," he whispered. "I know how much you love him. I'll drive you to his house."

"No." She pulled her arm out of his grasp. "This is goodbye, Luc. To borrow an expression your mother used with me, *'Adieu'.*"

Luc had no choice but to let her disappear out the door.

Until now he hadn't realized the depth of the damage he'd done.

By waiting to tell her about Paulette until after he'd come home with groceries that day, he'd given his mother the perfect opportunity to vent her pain in a way that had broken something inside Rachel.

Unfortunately she'd come home to another nightmare.

Much as he wanted to go after her, he would have to wait until her grandfather had passed away and she'd managed to work through some of her grief.

CHAPTER EIGHT

RACHEL slipped out the rear door of the restaurant where deliveries were made. At the end of the alley she hailed a taxi and went straight to her grandfather's.

Finding Luc in her office had shocked her so much, she'd had to get out of there.

Hearing about the loss of their baby and Paulette's tragic situation had turned Rachel inside out.

Surely Luc didn't believe they would pick up where they'd left off just because he'd finally told her the truth about his life—

Rachel felt as if the night they'd spent together had happened to someone else on a different planet. She couldn't relate to that Rachel who'd begged and pleaded with Luc to let her help him secure his vines. Anything to get closer to him.

Anger and humiliation swept over her to realize she was the one who'd thrown herself at him. She had no one but herself to blame.

It was because of her weakness for him that he'd flown to London. By confiding in her, he thought that was all it would take before she went running back into his arms again while he waited for his wife to recover.

Why not? Rachel had offered herself up as a feast for his delectation. He *was* a man after all.

And she was a woman who'd done something all stupid women had done since time immemorial.

But she only had to learn a painful lesson once before making the necessary changes.

Coming face to face with Luc this evening had put the seal on an idea that had been lurking since she'd given Max her notice.

"We're here, miss," the taxi driver called to her.

"So we are." Her mind had been so far away, she hadn't noticed the car had stopped.

She got out, paid the driver and rushed inside the mansion.

As she hurried up the stairs it struck her that one day soon she wouldn't find her grandfather here. All that would remain would be his four-story Georgian home full of memories.

More pain assailed her. It was too much on top of seeing Luc again. She was still trembling from their unexpected encounter.

When Rachel let herself inside her grandfather's room, the nurse was helping him drink water from a straw. Her slightly balding Uncle John stood on the other side of the bed encouraging his father to take his time between coughs.

The effort made her grandfather's lips tremble. She could tell he was weaker tonight.

Oh, Grandfather.

She fought tears before approaching the hospital bed that had been brought in.

"Look who's here, Father."

"Rachel," the old man's voice croaked.

John's blue-gray eyes welcomed her. "You're early tonight," he whispered.

"I couldn't stay away." In truth she couldn't run from Luc fast enough.

"Ivy came this afternoon and said he wasn't doing well. I decided not to go over to the restaurant."

Rachel was glad John's wife had been spending time with her grandfather. He enjoyed her.

"Rachel?" he muttered.

"You stay with him," John said in an aside. "Ivy's got dinner waiting for me downstairs."

Rachel nodded. After her uncle left the room with the nurse, she pulled the armchair next to the bed.

"I'm right here."

He opened his eyes to look at her. "Any word from your Frenchman?"

Her grandfather always got right down to the heart of the matter.

"H-he came to see me tonight at the restaurant."

"That doesn't surprise me. But it means you've sent him away. Otherwise you wouldn't be here."

"You're my only priority."

After a coughing spell he said, "Now you're telling me a lie."

Tears stung her eyelids. "Let's not talk about him." Never again. "How are you really feeling?"

"My solicitor asked me the same thing this morning. I told him I felt lousy."

She moaned inwardly. "You've done business today?"

"I told him to come by early when neither of my sons would be around. I added a codicil to my will."

"Grandfather—" A sob escaped before she rested her head on his arm.

"After I'm gone, I've instructed that this house be put up for sale. The proceeds will go equally to the three restaurants. What do you think?"

"It's the perfect solution to an insoluble problem."

He patted her head. Then she heard a deep sigh. "Now I have to work on a solution for your happiness," his voice trailed. He sounded exhausted.

Alarmed, she raised her head. "I'm fine. All you have to do is get better. Now go to sleep."

"I'm afraid to. It isn't time yet."

His admission killed her. By now the tears were streaming down her face.

A noise at the door brought her head around. In the aperture she saw the silhouette of her sister. A lighter brunette, more curvy than Rachel and almost as tall.

She advanced quietly into the room. The strong resemblance to their stunning mother shook Rachel.

Their eyes met for a soul-searching moment.

Rachel was too happy to talk. All she could do was hold out her hand.

Rebecca hurried forward and grasped it across their grandfather's chest.

As their fingers clung Rachel had the sudden feeling a miracle was happening.

Their grandfather's eyes opened. When he saw who it was, his countenance brightened in a way Rachel hadn't seen since before Lucia had become ill and died.

"Rebecca." There was a world of love in his voice. "God heard my prayers. My two beauties together at last."

"Hold on a moment, Mr Chartier."

Luc's hand tightened on his cell phone. He'd called *The Times* in London every day for ten days, waiting for news of an obituary.

"Yes. I have it here. William Valentine, ninety, passed away at home on June thirtieth, from a fatal embolism."

That was two days ago. Rachel would be inconsolable right now.

"Does it say where the funeral is going to be held?"

"Let me look. Yes. The family home at eleven a.m. on Friday the eighth of July."

"May I have the address please."

When she'd given it to him, he thanked her and hung up.

The eighth was still days away. Undoubtedly they'd been forced to wait until all the family members could be in attendance.

Luc wouldn't be among the mourners, but there was something he could do. For that he needed Giles.

When he reached Thann, he found him in one of the cellars of the convent taking inventory.

"Salut, mon vieux."

Giles turned his head. "Luc—I didn't know you were coming today."

"Something has happened you should know about. I wanted to talk to you in person."

The old man straightened. "Any more signs that Paulette is waking up?"

"No. The doctor has done every test. Despite her eyes opening, she's still in a vegetative state." After a pause, "The Brouets are still hopeful."

Giles eyed him shrewdly. "But you aren't."

"I don't know. To be frank, I dread my visits now. When her eyes were closed, I could still imagine them alive and flashing."

He rubbed the back of his neck. "That vacant stare chills my blood."

"That's because her spirit's gone."

Silence filled the cellar.

"You think I've been a fool?"

"What I think doesn't matter. You're the one who hasn't been able to forgive yourself for her accident."

The older man sighed. "You know something, Luc? If everyone went around taking on guilt for something they didn't do, we would all qualify as *idiots*."

That was what Rachel's grandfather had told her over the impasse with her sister. It was so easy to see how to solve the problem when it was someone else's.

"One more thing, Luc."

Apparently Giles wasn't finished. "If you continue to avoid Rachel out of guilt, then I don't mind calling you an *imbécile* to your face."

Giles was nothing if not brutally honest.

"If I'm avoiding her, it's for a very good reason. Her grandfather just died."

The old man shook his head sadly. "She loved her *grand-père*."

"I know. He made up for her father's inadequacies." Without him, she was going to feel lost.

"The funeral's on Friday. Let's send a spray of pink roses from you, Solange and the company. Will you do the honors?"

He handed him the paper with the address of the Valentine home. Giles nodded and slipped it in his pocket. "I'll take care of it."

"*Merci.* I can always count on you. If you need me, I'm on my way to Mulhouse."

"What's in Mulhouse?"

It was the same question he'd asked Rachel.

"Let's just say I'm looking for a peace offering."

"For your *maman*?"

Giles knew everything that went on in the Chartier household. "No. Not for her."

Luc had a penchant for Greek history. When they wanted to conquer Troy, they presented them a gift at the gates.

On Thursday morning Rachel awakened with a sick, basal skull headache. The kind that always heralded the onset of her period.

When she counted back, she realized her last period had ended around the twenty-eighth of May, over a week before she'd left for France.

With her life in painful chaos, she hadn't realized until now how late it was.

Once years ago, after moving to the UK following her college graduation, she hadn't had a period for ten months.

It had frightened her that she might have developed endometriosis like her poor sister, who'd been plagued with female problems. But the doctor had told her it was because she'd gone to a different climate.

Sometimes relocation or emotional upheaval affected the menstrual cycle. He'd given her a shot to bring on her period. Since then she'd never been late.

Needing some painkillers and a shower in that order, Rachel climbed out of bed and staggered to the bathroom, realizing her experience with Luc and the death of her grandfather had turned her inside out and thrown her off schedule.

But she received a real jolt when she checked and discovered there was no sign of her period.

Nothing but the headache.

If she called her doctor, the first thing he would ask after offering his condolences was, "Have you been sexually active?"

For the first time in her life she would have to say yes.

One night out of all the nights of her life.

"Did you take precautions?"

Rachel gripped the sink for support.

No. No precautions. What had happened had been unplanned on both their parts. Their needs had taken over so completely, rational thought had ceased to exist.

Rachel looked at herself in the mirror. Was it possible? Or was her pain responsible for her body being out of whack?

When her cell phone rang, she jumped. It was probably Emma. They were planning to meet at the mansion and start making food. After the funeral and interment tomorrow, the family would be coming back to the house to eat.

She hurried into the bedroom and checked the caller ID. It was her father, always in crisis.

"Dad?"

"I need you at the restaurant as soon as you can get here."

"But we're not going to be open until next Monday."

In honor of her grandfather, John had made the decision that the restaurants would be closed from Wednesday through Sunday.

"Somebody has to keep Bella Lucia running behind the scenes."

She shook her head. No one bought his martyr act, least of all Rachel.

"The shipment of Chartier wines has arrived."

A groan sounded in her throat.

Just hearing Luc's name made her heart beat so fast, it was unhealthy.

The shipment couldn't have come at a worse emotional time for Rachel, yet her father was oblivious to her pain.

"I've called in the stock boys and want you to oversee their work while they take it off the truck. Since you're the one who ordered it, you'd better make certain Chartier et Fils hasn't short-changed us."

Luc would never do that. But her father's mood was so volatile since her grandfather had died, everyone was giving him wide berth.

"As soon as I get dressed, I'll be over."

This close to the funeral she didn't dare cross him for fear she'd push him over the edge.

Besides, something else much more serious than placating her father was eating her alive.

What if the impossible had happened? What if she was one of those women whose fertile time was different from the average female?

Heaven knew she suffered for Rebecca who'd always had female problems. Rachel was her twin.

What if…?

She covered her mouth, traumatized by the implication.

An ad she'd seen on TV popped into her mind. A new product that could detect pregnancy earlier than ever.

On her way to the restaurant, she would stop at the pharmacy and buy a kit.

She didn't really believe she could be pregnant, but a negative test result would relieve her so she could make it through the funeral without falling apart.

During the next hour she found out there were increasing degrees of torture. The rack couldn't have been more agonizing than having to examine each case of Riesling and Tokay.

The memories of Luc suffocated her, adding to her grief, which was all part of one dark pit when she considered she might have conceived his child. She couldn't leave the wine room fast enough.

When she walked in her father's office to give him a full account, she discovered him opening a package sitting on his desk.

He flashed her a quick glance. "You didn't tell me you'd sent me a present from Mulhouse."

She shook her head. "I didn't."

"Then what's this? The note Max left said it was delivered by courier yesterday afternoon."

He pulled three miniature classic model cars from the pellets.

Her heart started to thud. Luc— He'd done it.

No-o-o.

"I—I forgot about that," she dissembled.

"I guess you did." He studied them with pleasure. "How did you know which ones to pick?"

How had Luc known? Why had Luc done this? It couldn't possibly change anything.

"I—I'm glad you like them."

She put the bills of lading on his desk. "Every bottle of wine arrived intact."

"Excellent," he murmured while he was still admiring the green model.

"Dad? I have to leave. There's a lot to do before the funeral."

He stood up. "I'll drive us back to the mansion. John thinks he's in charge of the whole damn funeral, but I've got news for him. Let's go."

She'd put the item she'd purchased inside her purse. During the drive, she gripped it so tightly, her knuckles turned white.

Once they reached the mansion, she dashed upstairs to the bathroom off the ante-room.

After she'd done the test, she went into the bedroom, terrified to look at it.

Knowing Emma was downstairs waiting for her, Rachel finally found the courage to see what was there.

At the first glance, her body broke out in a cold sweat.

"Rachel?"

When she heard the sound of Rebecca's voice, the plastic apparatus fell from her hand. She scrambled to pick it up, but the motion made her so dizzy, she had to sit down on the bed.

Rebecca rushed over to her. "What's wrong? You're as white as a sheet. Sit still. I'll get it."

"No—" Rachel cried, but it was too late. Rebecca had already plucked the test from the floor.

Eyes wide with shock, she handed it to Rachel. "Oh…Rachel. I'm sorry to have walked in on you. I wasn't sure you were even in here, but the door was open. Emma thought you'd come in. I told her I'd find you."

Rachel was still fighting dizziness.

"Don't apologize. Please don't. There's been so much pain in this family, I couldn't stand for there to be any more.

"I—I've just found out I'm pregnant, and I don't know what to do." She broke down sobbing.

Rebecca sat down on the bed and pulled her into her arms. She rocked her like a baby. It seemed the most natural thing in the world even though they'd spent so many years apart.

"Oh, Rebecca—" She hugged her back, needing her sister terribly.

"It's going to be all right, Rachel. I'm in love, too, but the whole thing's impossible so I recognize all the signs."

"Mitch Tucker?"

"Yes, but I don't want to talk about him. Tell me about this man who's the father of my niece or nephew."

"I wouldn't know where to begin."

"Just start at the beginning. We used to tell each other everything. Remember?"

"As if I could forget." She finally let go of her. "I've missed you more than you'll ever know. I should never have let Dad's needs influence me to stay in the UK.

"Forgive me for not being there to help more with Mom at the end. I loved her with all my heart and would have come before she died, but Dad insisted I go on that business trip with him.

"He was afraid for me to fly home in case I decided to stay. He's impossible to live with if you fight him on anything."

"I know," Rebecca whispered. "The trouble was, Mom was so bitter about the divorce, I was torn and felt her pain. Many times I wanted to fly to London to be with you, but I knew it would hurt her, and I didn't think Dad would approve. He preferred you to me."

Rachel shook her head. "Only because I felt Dad was more vulnerable than Mom because of his inadequacies, and he capitalized on it.

"The truth is, they were two angry, needy people, Rebecca. We were caught in the middle. After college I admit I wanted to spend time with him, but the price was too high. I saw less and less of Nana and Poppy, whom I adored. But the worst was the rift it caused between you and me."

She smiled tearfully at her sister. "I've always loved you, Rebecca. I just didn't know how to fix it."

Rebecca choked down a sob. "Neither did I. In the beginning I felt like you betrayed me and Mom. After Mom died, I felt isolated and alone. I kept hoping Dad would send for me, but he didn't. It was either wallow in pain, or make the most of my career."

"Rebecca—Dad is incapable of a healthy relationship with anyone."

"I agree, but it has taken me years to figure it out. Too long. Oh, Rachel, I'm so glad you called me to come. It gave me this precious time with Grandfather."

Rachel wiped the tears off her sister's face. "He loved you so much and died happy because you came. I can tell you he always grieved over the divorce and our father's inability to understand that you and I should never have been split up."

"Well, we're together now."

"And we'll never let anything separate us again, even if we work thousands of miles away from each other."

A look of compassion entered Rebecca's blue eyes. "So now tell me about the man you're in love with."

Rachel needed no urging to reveal it all. When she'd finished, her sister got up from the bed to look down at her.

"I don't care if his ex-wife lies in that coma for another ten years. Luc has a right to know he's going to be a father again.

"With my disease, I doubt I'll ever be able to have children. They're a gift, Rachel. You don't know how lucky you are.

"Go to him and tell him the truth. That's all you need to do. The rest will take care of itself. He helped make that baby. You can't hold that back from him. If Grandfather were still alive, he'd tell you the same thing."

Rachel nodded. Her eyes darted to the *Black Beauty* book he'd given her. She'd brought it from the flat to show him she still had her treasured gift.

She reached for it. "Do you still have your book, Rebecca?"

Her sister gasped softly. "I—I brought *Sleeping Beauty* with me when I stopped in New York for my passport. I don't know why I did. It's at Stephanie's."

Rachel smiled sadly. "I think we both wanted to feel closer to him. But you know something? He gave us the wrong books.

"You're the true equestrian in the family. I'm afraid I was always dreaming of a far-away kingdom and a prince who would take me to his castle and love me and only me for ever."

She set it on the bed. "Now it's time to put childish things away."

"You're right, sister dear," Rebecca said softly. "We have a funeral to help plan."

With their arms around each other's waists, they left the bedroom in search of Emma.

* **

When it came time to put a flower on their grandfather's silver-blue casket, Rachel sought Rebecca's gaze. By tacit agreement they both got up from the chairs. Clasping hands, they walked beneath the graveside canopy to his final resting place.

"We're together, Grandfather," Rachel whispered.

"You don't have to worry about your two beauties any more," Rebecca said in a hushed voice. "Be happy with Grandmother."

Tears trembled on Rachel's lashes. "When you see our mother, tell her we love her."

Rebecca squeezed her hand before they both placed a white rose on the lid of the coffin.

Maybe it was because they were twins and could read each other's minds. Whatever it was, no words needed to be said for them to head to the black limo they'd come in.

The driver started up the motor and drove them back to the mansion.

"Look—" Rachel cried out when she saw a huge spray of pink roses on a stand in the dining room. "Those must have arrived too late to go to the cemetery with the other flowers."

"They're absolutely breathtaking." Rebecca walked over to read the enclosed card.

She took so long, Rachel said, "Whoever sent them must have been a very close friend of Grandfather's."

Wordlessly Rebecca handed it to her.

Mystified by her behavior, Rachel read the inscription.

Rachel— If Louis were still alive, he would have wanted to send these flowers in remembrance of a friendship forged through a mutual love of the fruit of the vine. Ironic that it took place during a time of war.

William Valentine will live in all our hearts as we know he lives in yours.

With great affection, Giles, Solange, Luc and the family of Chartier et Fils.

Rebecca came to stand behind Rachel. She put her hands on her shoulders.

"You do know you have to tell him."

Yes, Rachel did know, but not for a while. There was something she had to do first. She and Rebecca had talked about it.

When Wednesday came around and Rachel couldn't find Max in his office, she headed for the kitchen.

Sure enough she discovered him and Emma with their heads together. No doubt they were talking about their father's eruption upon learning the contents of the codicil to their grandfather's will.

Under the circumstances, Rachel had no compunction about following through with certain decisions she'd made. Her reconciliation with Rebecca had given her the strength to do what she had to do.

"Is this a private conversation, or can anyone join in?" she teased.

Both heads turned in her direction.

"Feel free," Max said with a smile. "One guess what we're talking about."

Max could take care of himself. But Emma looked worried. Rachel had always felt protective of her younger half sister, and never more so than now.

"What are you doing at the restaurant this early?" he asked.

She switched her gaze to him. "I've come to say goodbye, and thought I'd do it before everyone reports for work." Mainly their father who wouldn't be arriving for at least three more hours.

Emma blinked. "Where are you going?"

"You haven't told her yet?" she asked Max.

He folded his arms. "Come on, Rachel. You didn't really mean it."

She nodded. "Yes, I really did. I've already cleaned out my office. It's ready for the new wine buyer, whoever he or she is."

"You're leaving Bella Lucia?" Emma cried out, aghast.

"Yes. I'm going into restaurant management."

Emma shook her head. "At the restaurant in Mayfair or Knightsbridge?"

"Neither."

Emma looked absolutely bewildered. "What do you mean?"

"I'm leaving Bella Lucia for good. I have tentative appointments to talk to some restaurant owners in New York. Rebecca and I decided we'd like to live closer together."

She saw a glimmer of approval in Max's eyes. "Good for you."

"I'll be posting a letter of explanation to Dad when I leave here in a few minutes. He'll get it tomorrow or the next day."

At Emma's look of dismay she said, "Don't worry. As soon as I'm situated, I'll phone both of you and let you know where I am and what I'm doing. There's a realtor who's in charge of subletting my flat until I know what I want to do with it."

"I'm going to miss you so much." Emma threw her arms around Rachel.

"It's going to be a wrench for me too, Emma. I've loved working with you and Max. But Rebecca and I need to catch up on years of separation, and with Grandfather gone…"

Suddenly she was dissolved in tears that always threatened these days.

After hugging Max, she started to leave, but he called her back. Rachel turned around. "What is it?"

"Since Emma is too modest to tell you, then I will."

"Tell me what?"

"Oh, I'll do it," Emma muttered. "Unbelievable as this may sound, I've been commissioned to be the head chef for a coronation taking place in Meridia in the near future."

Rachel flashed her a tender smile. "That's not unbelievable, Emma. It's long past time your talents were lauded internationally. A coronation will be a huge media event. You'll become more famous than you already are."

"That's what I was saying," Max chimed in.

"Who's being crowned?"

"Prince Sebastian."

"Whoa…the playboy all Europe has been talking about? Hmm… Interesting…"

"Oh, stop—" Emma cried, but her cheeks were flushed.

"No— I won't," Rachel persisted. "We've served a lot of royals here from around the world. One of the Meridian royal family must have tasted some of your superb meals and put your name on their secret short list."

"Isn't that just what I said?" Max blurted.

In a quieter voice Rachel said, "No doubt Dad is walking around like *he* has been made king."

The three of them burst into laughter.

"Seriously, Emma. Out of all the great chefs in the world, his very own daughter has attained a singular honor. I'm so proud of you.

"You can bet I'll be phoning you constantly for a blow-by-blow account of every exciting detail."

Max nodded. "That goes for me, too, Emma,"

Rachel stared at the two of them. "I really am going to miss both of you. Take care…"

Before Rachel broke down again, she hurried out of the kitchen and left the restaurant on foot.

Once she reached her flat, she called for a taxi to take her to the airport for her flight to New York.

Besides starting a new career, she would call Rebecca's ob-gyn for a complete check-up. Pending the outcome—because it was still hard to believe she was pregnant—she would inform Luc.

CHAPTER NINE

Luc couldn't believe it was already August eighth, and not a personal word from Rachel.

One month ago today had been her grandfather's funeral. The Valentine family had sent a printed thank-you note for the flowers in care of Chartier et Fils. That was it.

After what she'd shared with him at his house about the dynamics in her family, Luc knew how hard William's death would have been on her. But she could have no conception of what her silence was doing to him.

At the conclusion of a business lunch with a first-time buyer from Norway, he excused himself and left for the St Hippolyte winery. On the way, he finally gave in to the impulse to phone her cell. But he received a shock to discover her service had been disconnected.

Alarmed by that piece of news, he called information for the number of the Bella Lucia on King's Road.

This abstinence out of respect for her pain had gone on long enough.

"Yes?"

The person who answered sounded young and out of breath. Luc checked his watch. It was two-thirty here, which made it one-thirty in London. Probably one of the staff had picked up, since the restaurant didn't open until five.

"I need to speak to your wine buyer. This is an urgent call."

"I don't think he's come in yet, but I'll check."

Luc frowned. "I'm talking about Rachel Valentine."

"Oh. She doesn't work here anymore."

Luc stood on his brakes. "Is she at one of the other Bella Lucias?"

"No. She lives in New York now."

He cursed under his breath. "Does someone at the restaurant have her new number?"

"I don't know. Call back tonight when we're open. I've got to go. Sorry."

Luc would do better than that. As soon as he'd given Giselle the order from their newest buyer, he'd stop by the hospital to see Paulette, then fly to London this evening and speak to Rachel's father in person. The man kept a thumb on his daughter and could tell Luc what he needed to know.

Since their excruciatingly painful encounter in London, he couldn't sleep, couldn't concentrate. Until he could see her again and they could really talk without interruption, he'd remain in this nightmarish limbo, unable to go backward or forward. Much more of this and—

He stopped right there because his thoughts were too black.

Upon entering the parking area surrounding the winery, he noticed every space taken by tourists.

Though on some level it pleased him that business was flourishing, he couldn't summon the old excitement he'd once felt for just being alive.

This wasn't living.

Giselle had been right about that. Existence wasn't enough, but fate had been serving him up a belly full of it. He'd be damned if he was going to keep on swallowing it to the last dreg.

No sooner had he driven around the back to let himself in his private entrance than his cell phone rang. It was the hospital. He assumed Yves was in Paulette's room and needed to talk.

He clicked on and said hello.

"Monsieur Chartier? This is Louise."

His favorite upbeat nurse, but she sounded subdued, which was very unlike her.

"Yes, Louise?"

"I'm so sorry to have to tell you this when you've been praying for a miracle. I'm afraid Paulette died a few minutes ago."

What?

"She died?" he whispered incredulously.

A shock wave passed through his body. His thoughts reeled as his whole life with her suddenly flashed before his eyes.

He barely had the presence of mind to stop the car before it ran into the wall.

"Did the family ask for the machines to be shut off?" He'd thought they'd had an understanding.

"No, no. Her lungs unexpectedly filled with pneumonia. It happened after my second-to-last check on her. When I came in at the end of my shift, she was gone."

Tears trickled from his eyes.

So now you're free, chérie. I have my answer.

Paulette had left this world with the machines still going. She hadn't wanted to wait until the harvest.

It was over.

Silent sobs shook his body. He fought for control. "Has the family been notified?"

"Yes."

He wiped his eyes. "I'll be right over. Thank you, Louise. I'll always be indebted to you and the staff for the impeccable care you've given her all this time."

"It was our privilege." Now she was in tears. "I can't tell you how sorry we all are."

"That's very kind. A month ago Giles told me her spirit had left her body. In my heart I think I knew it was true, but I wanted to give it until the end of the summer."

"You did everything possible and more. We all admire you. So often I've wondered how you've managed when I know how much you suffered. You're a very strong man to have endured this much pain. *Que Dieu vous bénisse, Luc.*"

Everything passed in a blur as he rushed to the hospital. He found Father Pourdras in the room surrounded by the Brouet relatives. The priest who'd married him and Paulette had started a prayer over her body now covered by a sheet.

"The Lord giveth, and the Lord taketh away…"

* * *

The doctor had confirmed Rachel was pregnant and that her due date was March the third.

After she left his office, she realized she couldn't put off telling Luc any longer.

The manager of the restaurant where she was training had been nice enough to give her time off for personal leave.

Two days later she flew to Paris, and from there to Colmar where she'd booked a hotel.

If Luc joined her at an obscure little restaurant in the town, they could talk without fear of someone recognizing him. Rachel didn't want word getting back to Madame Chartier that her son was still carrying on a clandestine affair with her.

But Rachel soon came to find out that the best laid plans didn't always work out.

After she checked in the Deux Couronnes Hotel, she called his cell phone from the phone in her room. If she used her new cell, he would be forewarned by seeing her name on the caller ID.

Rachel wanted the element of surprise on her side in order to feel she was in control. But the surprise rebounded on her because, instead of picking up, he'd left his voice mail on.

She debated what to do. It wasn't as if she were on a buying trip and could set her own time schedule.

In the end, she called him again, this time on her cell, and told him she needed to see him as soon as possible. It was urgent. Would he please call her.

At a loose end and frustrated because it had taken her so long to gather the courage to phone him in the first place, she left the hotel to do some exploring.

The Deux Couronnes sat along one of the many canals of the Petite Venice area. Myriad cobblestoned streets gave the impression she'd entered a bygone age.

She was once again charmed by the many treasures of Alsace, and it came to her that all this beauty would be part of her baby's heritage. Now that she'd been to the doctor, her pregnancy had become real to her.

Was it a little half-French boy or girl who was tucked in behind her flat stomach? She wouldn't know the answer to that question for another couple of months.

By the time it was getting dark, he still hadn't phoned and she was exhausted. The doctor had told her exercise was good, but she'd probably overdone it.

Indescribably disappointed not to have heard from him, she returned to the hotel and ate a quick dinner.

Maybe he was on vacation, though she doubted it with Paulette in the hospital.

The most likely reason for his silence was a heavy workload. His schedule included entertaining clients who kept him busy at all hours.

A case in point was her own arrival in Thann on her first visit to Alsace. He'd taken her on a personal tour of his vineyards after normal working hours.

Her body throbbed just thinking about her intense attraction to him. It was an experience she would never forget in more ways than one.

That night had led to another magical night, followed by a month so black, she was surprised she was still alive. And pregnant…

She needed to tell Luc in person that she was nurturing their baby.

But if he didn't call her tomorrow, then the next best thing she could do was write him a letter. If she posted it from Colmar, he would realize she'd tried to see him in person before returning to the States.

As she got in bed and began composing it in her mind, she heard a distinct knock on her door.

"Rachel?"

Her heart gave a great leap.

Luc! He was here? Now?

"I—I didn't expect you tonight." But she should have known he'd come. He possessed that sixth sense necesssary to a success-ful vintner. Once he'd seen the hotel's phone number on his caller ID, he'd put two and two together.

"You said it was urgent. Let me in," he insisted in that deep voice that brooked no argument.

"Just a minute."

She'd thought he'd caused her enough pain that her feelings for him had been burned out of her.

Not so.

The thrill of hearing his voice overwhelmed her. But following that reaction she felt apprehension. Now that the moment was here, she had no idea how he would react to the news that he was going to be a father. Again.

Rebecca had advised her to just tell him the truth, and the rest would take care of itself. But Rachel knew it wasn't that simple. He was still waiting for Paulette to wake up so he could try to put their marriage back together.

Rachel threw off her nightgown and slipped into jeans and a top.

"Shall I open it for you?"

"No—I'm coming."

Rachel was all thumbs as she unlocked the door. At the sound of the click, he pushed it open.

The first thing she noticed was his formal attire. He was in a black suit and tie, she'd never seen him look more devastatingly handsome. But when she stared up at his face, she noticed he was leaner and wore a hunted expression. The lines around his mouth were more pronounced.

Her hand went to her throat in alarm. "When I told you it was urgent, I didn't mean you had to tear yourself away from an important dinner party."

His veiled gaze assessed her features with unsettling intensity before he moved into the room. She backed away to keep distance between them, sensing there was something vitally different about him.

He shut the door, still keeping his eyes leveled on her.

"There was a funeral today. Paulette died on the eighth."

Rachel stood there like a victim of shellshock.

"W-what took her?"

"Pneumonia. Her family buried her this afternoon. I had just left their house to go home when I checked my messages."

"Luc—" she cried, utterly horrified that she'd intruded on the most painful day of his life.

She shook her head. "I had no way of knowing."

"You think I don't realize that?"

Her eyes filmed over. "I'm so terribly sorry. I can't imagine the agony you're going through."

"Not agony, Rachel. I've had three years to come to terms with her death."

After a long silence he said, "The kind you're talking about happened when Paulette lost touch with reality."

He rubbed the side of his jaw where she could see the shadow of his beard.

"It must have been devastating."

She'd had a month for his revelations to sink in. He'd been living through a horrific experience.

"It was."

He shed his suit jacket and tie. They landed on the end of the bed. She watched him undo the top buttons of his shirt, as if he needed more freedom to breathe.

"Another man I could have dealt with. But her mental state…"

His dark glance pierced through to her soul.

"Rachel—I swear it was never my intention to keep secrets from you."

"I believe you," she murmured, grabbing the chair for support.

But there was one truth Rachel couldn't get past. Luc had loved Paulette. He'd wanted her back enough to wait three years for her to wake up. He'd paid his hard-earned money to fight Paulette's parents in court for the right to keep the machines on.

He and Paulette would still be happily married if their baby hadn't died. You didn't get over a love like theirs.

That was the kind of love Rachel wanted for herself. But she would never find it here.

Maybe in New York.

Maybe not.

She'd lost her heart to Luc. How could she ever give it to anyone else?

But it wasn't the same for him. He'd been at his lowest ebb when Rachel had begged him to love her. It had been a moment out of time that shouldn't have happened.

How unfair was life that she could get pregnant during one

careless night of passion outside the bonds of marriage? And his poor wife had been forced to wait three years for a baby they had both wanted so desperately, and ultimately lost.

She felt strong hands close over her shoulders. "You've listened to me long enough. Now I need to know what was so urgent, you came all the way from New York to see me."

"How did you know I'd moved there?"

"Someone at the restaurant told me."

"Dad?"

"No," he declared in a note of finality. "What's in New York?"

Grasping for a plausible answer, she said, "The rest of my life."

He turned her around so she was forced to face him. More lines marred his striking features.

"There's nothing left for you in England with your grandfather gone. Is that it?" he asked in a silky voice.

His dark eyes threw out a probing challenge that made her shiver.

"It's more than that, Luc, but this isn't a good time to discuss it. However I do want to thank you for the funeral spray. Everyone in the family said the flowers were the most beautiful pink roses they'd ever seen.

"And the model cars. Your gift delighted my father, which was an amazing feat since it's almost impossible to please him."

"I'm glad." His hands kneaded her upper arms through the material of her top, heating her skin. "Now tell me why you're really here. The last word from your lips was *adieu.*"

"I know." She averted her eyes.

Rachel was uncertain what to do. When she'd come here, she'd been on a mission.

But he'd just buried his wife earlier in the day. Tonight was *not* the time for him to find out he'd made Rachel pregnant.

Heavens—what was she saying? There was no good time for earth-shaking news like this.

He said her name again in a way that broke down her defenses, his breathing sounding ragged. "When you try to avoid me, you remind me of the demure maiden in a certain Italian painting hanging in the Uffizi I've admired.

"You both have flawless skin, but the touch of sadness in her is more pronounced in you. I realize losing your grandfather was traumatic."

"It's true I'm going to miss him…" her voice wobbled "…but he lived a long, full life and was eager to be with Grandmother, so in that sense it was easier to let him go."

His eyes played over her. It was hard to believe that instead of an ocean separating them, she was in touching distance of him. But she couldn't do this.

"Don't put me off any longer, Rachel. You came for a specific reason."

Floundering for an opening, she said, "Why don't we wait until tomorrow when we've both had some sleep?"

His eyes narrowed. "There'll be no sleep for me tonight, and I dare say not for you either. What's eating you alive?"

Her head flew back. She didn't know how to begin.

This was so much harder than she'd imagined it would be. Remarkable as he was, finding out he was going to be a father would throw his painful world into upheaval of a different kind.

She moistened her lips nervously. "I never meant to come back to Alsace."

"Tell me something I don't already know."

His barely leashed impatience caused her to take a step backward, but he didn't let her go altogether. His sensual mouth had thinned even more.

"I wish I could have saved us this moment, Luc, but some things in life have to be said in person. This is one of those times."

At those words, he relinquished his hold on her. His hands went to his hips in an undeniably male stance. He was waiting…

A nervous shiver raced through her body.

"All right, Rachel." He'd reached the end of his tolerance. "What's put the haunted shadows in those blue eyes? Just say it—"

She drew in a sharp breath. "I'm pregnant."

There was instant stillness before Luc's eyes blazed with a strange light.

"Say that again?"

She realized he needed time for his mind to wrap around

what she'd just told him. How well Rachel understood. It had taken her over a month to believe it herself.

"I realize it seems way too soon for me to know something this vital, Luc, but my period was late."

She bowed her head. "I haven't been late since my college days. At first I thought it was my worry over grandfather that had thrown my body off kilter.

"But on the outside chance that I could be pregnant, I took an early detection test." Her voice was shaking. "It came out positive, and two days ago my doctor in New York confirmed it. I'm expecting our baby March third."

"Rachel—"

She heard so much emotion in that one word, she couldn't tell what exactly he was feeling beyond total shock.

"Neither of us planned for this to happen. I blame no one but myself, and don't want anything from you.

"But I felt that before any more time passed, you needed to be told."

She buried her face in her hands. "Forgive me for coming on this terrible day. I can't believe my timing. But since we can't change that now, let me say one more thing."

She raised her head. "I speak from experience when I tell you that our baby will want your love if you want to give it. But it's going to be complicated because I live in New York and—"

"If I want to give it—" He cut her off angrily, not hearing the rest. *"Mon Dieu—"*

Rachel wasn't prepared when he crushed her against him. With every breath she tried to take, he molded her more firmly to his body.

"You're really carrying my child?"

"Yes."

Rachel couldn't formulate words. It felt like years since she'd been in his arms.

"Let me hold you for a minute while I get used to the idea that I made you pregnant."

He rocked her in place, kissing her cheeks and temple as if she were a cherished possession.

"To think our one night of loving resulted in a baby— You don't have any idea what this news means to me, Rachel." He pressed his face in her silky hair.

"Forget New York. You need care and waiting on. I lost one child. I'm not about to lose this one," he vowed, wrapping his strong arms more firmly around her.

Somewhere deep down she'd sensed Luc was the kind of man who would embrace fatherhood and all it meant. She knew he'd make a remarkable parent.

He was bigger than life. That was what made him such an extraordinary man.

No matter the circumstances, no matter the impact on his life, any son or daughter of his would know the depth of his love.

Their child wouldn't have to hang around waiting for his approbation, or beg for it. Luc would give it freely.

That was the only reason she'd been willing to face this crucible on his territory.

But before any more time passed, she needed to assure him that taking care of *her* wasn't his responsibility.

Slowly she tried to ease out of his arms, but he was too strong for her.

"Why are you pulling away from me?"

"Because we have to talk."

"I thought that's what we were doing."

"We are, but I can't forget that you've just come from burying your wife."

With those words she moved away from him. "I know how much you were hoping she'd wake up and I can't comprehend your pain. Three years of waiting. And then for it to turn out like this. It hurts me that I've intruded on your private time."

Emotion threatened to overwhelm her, but she steeled herself to continue. "I wanted to do the right thing by telling you about the baby. Now that you know, I have to leave in the morning. When I go into labor next spring, I'll phone you. Hopefully by then your pain won't be so raw, and we can discuss our baby's future.

"Now, if you don't mind, I'm exhausted and need sleep before I board that flight tomorrow."

He stared her down. "I'm the father of our baby. If you think I'm going to let you out of my sight now, then you don't know me at all."

"You don't know me either—" she cried. His possessive tone made it difficult for her to keep her head on straight.

"That's the problem. Luc. We didn't spend more than five days together. We're practically strangers, yet we created a child while your wife was still in the hospital. We can't do this! *I* can't do it."

"What can't you do?" he demanded.

"I have a job in New York. If I stay here any longer, people will talk. Your mother will find out I was here on the night of Paulette's funeral. What would her family say if they knew you'd come to this hotel straight from their house?"

"I don't give a damn what anyone thinks. None of it will matter anyway when they find out we're married."

"Married? But we're not!"

"We're going to be."

Her face paled. "Surely you're joking."

Luc shook his head. "I've never been more serious in my life.

"Tomorrow I'll fly to New York with you. We'll get married civilly and take care of what needs to be done before coming home to live."

She stood there reeling in disbelief. "I couldn't possibly marry you. Everyone would go into shock. Your mother and Paulette's family would despise me."

"When they remember that Paulette divorced me three years ago. they'll get over it. Even if they don't—" He shrugged his broad shoulders. "We're going to be parents in a little less than seven months, so this isn't about us anymore, Rachel. A new life is growing inside you. It puts everything that's gone on before in the past where it belongs.

"This baby is our future. Our child deserves everything we have to give. That includes my name and my constant companionship."

Rebecca's words kept swirling in Rachel's head. *Tell him the truth… The rest will take care of itself.*

"No child of ours is going to be torn apart because I live on one continent and you on another.

"Look what that kind of arrangement did to you and your sister."

Rachel had no comeback for his logic. He'd managed to touch on that core of pain where he knew she'd been the most vulnerable.

One dark brow dipped ominously. "History's not going to repeat itself where our child is concerned. There'll be no divorce. We'll stay married, Rachel."

She knew those weren't empty words. Luc was an all-or-nothing man. It was the way he was made. That was one of the reasons she loved him so much.

But he didn't love her. To commit herself to him under these circumstances meant she'd be missing out on the one thing she'd hoped to find in life.

"Luc—I agree our child shouldn't have to travel back and forth on visitation, so I'm willing to move to Alsace after the baby's born.

"Ever since I flew here on my first trip, I made up my mind that one day I'd buy a little house in one of the villages. At the time I was thinking years down the road…but my pregnancy has changed the timetable. If I found a property somewhere in the province, then you could see the baby all the time without it disrupting your work"

His expression darkened like the thunderhead in the storm that had propelled her into his arms.

"Forget it, Rachel. If you're that worried about what people will think, then we'll live in New York."

Panic set in. "Don't be ridiculous. You're a vintner."

"I'll open a distributorship to expand Chartier wines on the North American continent. All that really matters is that we give our child a stable home life with a mother and father under one roof."

"It's *not* all that matters," she retorted, because he refused to consider any other alternative. "We both know your mother's not going to welcome me."

"Then it's her loss." He reached for her hand and clung to it. "I'm aching to be a father who takes turns getting up in the night to tend to our son or daughter.

"When the doctor told me our baby didn't make it, I felt

something die inside of me. But just now I came back to life when you told me we're expecting a baby."

Unaware of his own strength, he tightened his fingers around hers, giving her physical evidence of the magnitude of emotion driving him.

"You'll never want for anything and I promise to look after you and our child for as long as I live. You'll have no regrets— I'll make sure of it. I need to be a father to our baby, and I need you there to help me. Don't deny me that joy."

When she felt his lips kiss her forehead, her heart let out a little death gasp.

For better or for worse, she would have to take this man for her lawfully wedded husband. Now that he'd borne his soul to her, she couldn't possibly do anything else.

He finally released her, then paused at the door. "I'm leaving so you can get some sleep, but I'll be back in the morning to drive us to the airport. Considering you came to me as soon as you could, I'm confident you're not going to disappear on me. *Dors bien, ma belle.*"

Knowing his family wouldn't be in bed yet, Luc drove to his mother's home and let himself in the back door.

He was glad to discover the adults congregated around the kitchen table drinking coffee. While the women talked, Jean-Marc dipped the end of his baguette in the hot liquid before devouring it.

The second Luc's grieving mother saw him, she got up.

"I was hoping you would come over. We've been trying to reach you on the phone." Her arms went around him. "Where did you go after you left the Brouets'? I've been worried sick about you."

"Do you want coffee?" Giselle piped up, anticipating that he wouldn't like their mother fussing over him after a day like today. But this was one time his sister needn't have worried. Their mother's question had given him the perfect opening.

"*Non, merci,* Giselle."

He guided his mother back to her chair. After she sat down, he kept his hands on the back of one of the empty chairs.

"I've just come from Colmar."

Three pairs of dark eyes fastened on him in surprise. He could read their minds with ease.

"Rachel Valentine was there."

As his mother gasped he saw Giselle give her husband a secret look.

"I'm flying to New York with her in the morning. That means you're in charge, Jean-Marc."

While his brother-in-law stared at him in astonishment, his mother erupted on cue.

"Have you lost your mind, *mon fils?* Does she have no scruples? You just buried Paulette. I absolutely forbid you to go anywhere with that woman!"

"Be careful what you say, *Maman*. When we come back from our trip, that woman will be Madame Lucien Chartier, your new daughter-in-law."

At the stunned expression on her face he added, "We're expecting a baby on the third of March. You're going to be its *grand-mère*."

Giselle pushed herself away from the table and ran around to hug him.

"I'm so happy for you I could burst!"

"I knew I could count on you," he whispered.

Jean-Marc nodded at him with genuine affection. "Congratulations, Luc. I'm very happy for you. Does Giles know?"

"Not yet."

"The news is sure to please him. He said if you let her escape, he would marry Mademoiselle Valentine himself, if he were younger and she would have him."

Luc smiled. He knew the old man had a crush on her.

"Jean-Marc? I need you to do me a favor."

"Anything."

"Rachel has been a wine buyer for a long time. Now that she's going to be my wife, I'd like you to teach her about the family business. Everything. She's smart, and a fast learner. But the invitation is going to have to come from you and Giselle so she'll feel a real part of our family."

His mother shot to her feet. Anger had replaced her tears.

"If you marry her, you're going to alienate everyone who knows us. After your father worked so hard to make the business what it is today, can you live with that on your conscience?"

"How can you be so cruel, *Maman?*" Giselle intervened. "Don't you know everyone who knows our family has been wondering why Luc didn't get on with his life years before now?

"No one has done anything wrong. Paulette's chemical imbalance caused her to lose her mind. Let's be honest about that. I don't know another man who was willing to go through what Luc did, and now that he's paid the price, it's his turn to live. When people find out he's married again and expecting a baby, they'll cheer for him."

Luc kissed his sister's cheek. "Thank you, *chère soeur.*"

"You think Paulette's family will cheer you?" his mother cried out.

He glanced at her. "I can't worry about that, *Maman*. I know Yves will support me. He never wanted Paulette hooked up to those machines in the first place.

"But be that as it may, Rachel and I have a son or daughter on the way. It's up to you if you want to be a part of its life.

"Rachel's mother died years ago, so you'll be its *only grand-mère.*"

Purposely leaving her with that bit of news to ponder during the sleepless hours of the night, he kissed her cheek before striding out of the house to his car.

CHAPTER TEN

"WOULD you like to make a detour to London and see your father? We could fly from there to Colmar."

Rachel sat next to Luc in the back of the taxi driving them to Kennedy airport.

She shook her head. "I'd rather tell him over the phone and let him get used to the idea."

"Then we'll do it now." He pulled out his cell.

She bit her lip. "I don't know—"

"I do," Luc asserted in that natural voice of command he wasn't aware of. "He'll always be possessive of you, Rachel, so the sooner he finds out you have a husband devoted to you, the better."

She let out an anxious sigh. "You're right."

"What's his number?"

When she told him, he punched the digits, then reached for her hand. This time he threaded his fingers through hers as he'd done at the doctor's office as if to say they were partners now and would face the world together.

She checked her watch. "It's three-thirty over there. He's probably home getting ready to go to work."

Rachel hoped he hadn't left for the restaurant yet. Once he got there, he was usually out of sorts.

"Hello, Mr Valentine? Luc Chartier here."

She held her breath while they exchanged greetings. Her gaze darted to the diamond ring and gold wedding band adorning her left hand. Luc had left nothing undone during their three-day whirlwind in New York.

"I'm glad you like our wines. It was my lucky day in more ways than one when Rachel came to Alsace, because this morning she did me the honor of becoming my wife. We wanted you to be the first to know. Here she is."

Luc kissed the side of her tender neck before handing her the phone, making it difficult for her to think with any coherency.

"H-hello, Dad?"

Her father had viewed her resignation from the restaurant as a betrayal. Since then he'd been so surly over the phone, their conversations had been reduced to brief, unsatisfactory exchanges where he'd railed against her uncle John.

"Damn if you aren't a cool customer. I knew there had to be a reason you didn't meet personally with Jacques Bulot. So when am I going to meet Luc?"

"We're flying to Paris in the next few hours, but we could change our plans and come to London instead."

"This weekend wouldn't be the best time for me. I've hired a solicitor to fight the codicil in Father's will. We're going to be closeted at the house for the next few days."

Rachel shuddered. She wanted no part of a fight her father couldn't win.

"I understand. Maybe next month you could fly to Alsace and we'll take you on a tour of Luc's vineyards."

Her new husband could read between the lines and took the phone from her.

"Harvest is an exciting time, Mr Valentine. We'll look forward to entertaining you when you come. In the meantime, be assured I plan to take perfect care of your gorgeous daughter."

She turned her head away to hide her tears. Luc was going to be the perfect husband. But she didn't want perfection. His love was what she craved.,.

By the time they boarded their flight to Paris, exhaustion had caught up with her. She slept most of the way, thankful to have Luc who looked after her every need. At eight that night they arrived in Colmar.

Her fatigue still great because of her pregnancy, she drifted in and out of sleep on the drive to the house.

"We're home, Sleeping Beauty," he whispered as he carried her from the car.

"You've mixed me up with my sister," her voice slurred.

"No." Luc chuckled. He placed her on the bed in his bedroom. "It's definitely you, *ma belle au forêt dormant.*"

"What does that mean?"

"Literally, my beauty of the sleeping forest. You look exactly like a picture of her in an old fairy tale. I can't decide which appellation I like better." He removed her shoes and drew the duvet over her.

"Other appellation?" she asked groggily.

"Um. Madame Lucien Chartier. If we have a daughter we'll have to change the name of the business to Chartier et Fille."

That was the last thought she remembered before she awakened the next morning alone on the bed still fully clothed.

She must have passed out on Luc. Rachel couldn't remember ever doing that before.

Light from a semi-cloudy sky had filtered into the room. Disoriented, she lifted her head to glance at the clock on the bedside table. It said eleven-thirty. She'd never slept for so long!

There was no sign to suggest that Luc had joined her during their wedding night. He must have slept in the basement bedroom.

In New York he'd gone to a hotel, insisting she'd get a better sleep alone in Rebecca's apartment.

If this was going to be a pattern…

Her heart lurched to think he might have gone to the winery this morning.

Had he eaten anything before leaving?

Her stomach was making growling sounds. Though she'd love some rolls and coffee, the doctor had told her to avoid stimulants, so she would have to settle for juice from now on.

She was tempted to pad down the hall to the kitchen right now, but, after the experience of his mother walking in on her unannounced, Rachel decided to get showered and dressed first.

Luc had put her two suitcases on the floor at the end of the bed. Once she'd found fresh underwear and clothes, she headed for the bathroom, anxious to remove her wrinkled blouse and skirt. After being on a plane, she always felt grubby.

As she entered the bathroom she noticed Luc had put out his toiletries. His yellow bathrobe hung on the door.

Unable to resist, she reached out to touch it and discovered it was damp. That meant he'd come in the bedroom while she'd been asleep, and not that long ago either. Maybe he was still here!

She hurriedly submitted herself to the spray and gave her hair a good shampoo.

Eager to see him, she towel-dried the wet strands, then brushed it before tying it back with a ribbon.

Once she'd put on jeans and a printed blue top, she went in the other room to get her sandals out of the other suitcase.

An application of lipstick and she was ready.

Halfway down the hall she heard voices. A little closer and Luc said, "Awake at last. Come in, Rachel, and meet my sister Giselle."

A slender, attractive woman with light brown hair rushed across the living room to greet her. She looked to be close to Luc's age and was almost as tall as Rachel.

She kissed her on both cheeks, exuding a warmth that seemed totally genuine.

"My husband and I were so excited to learn Luc had got married, we couldn't wait to come and meet you. I hope you don't mind."

"Of course not. I've been wanting to meet you too."

Luc gave Rachel's mouth a swift kiss. "Why don't you sit down with Giselle and get acquainted? I'll bring in some food. I happen to know you're starving."

He'd probably heard her stomach growling earlier. How embarrassing.

"Do you want cranberry or apple juice?"

"Apple sounds good. Thank you," she whispered before sitting on the couch with Giselle.

Friendly brown eyes smiled at her, displaying none of the hostility their mother had exhibited.

"Welcome to the family. I'm so excited. Luc told us you're expecting a baby in the spring. I'm pregnant again, too," she confided.

"How exciting for you!" Rachel blurted. Their children would be cousins almost the same age.

Giselle nodded. "It's perfect. This means we'll have to have two baby parties! My boys are seven and nine, so we need all new baby paraphernalia."

By now Luc had brought in a large tray of food. He placed it on the coffee-table before handing them plates.

With one dark brow quirked he eyed his sister. "Does Jean-Marc know about this yet?"

Rachel couldn't help staring at him because he looked and sounded so happy. It made him seem younger and more carefree. She'd never seen Luc like this before.

"Yes. I told him last night. He's outside in your vineyard explaining everything to Patrick and Guy."

She grinned at Rachel. "You know how farmers always use the birth of a new calf or foal to explain reproduction to their children?"

Rachel nodded.

"Well, Jean-Marc's method is a little different. Right now he's telling them how the grape seed is implanted in the soil and soon a baby grape vine will poke its little head up."

Luc threw his head back in a burst of laughter. "Your husband and my wife have a lot in common."

He darted Rachel a devilish smile. It caused heat to fill her cheeks. To embarrass her further, Luc proceeded to tell his sister about a certain conversation in a certain vineyard in Thann.

While they ate, Giselle winked at Rachel. "Giles said you had a feeling for the vine beyond the ordinary person. Have you thought about what you'll do now that you're not going to be buying wines for your family business?"

Rachel finished the last of her juice. "Actually we've been so busy, that's one subject we haven't touched on yet."

"Good, because I have an idea." Giselle set down her plate. "How would you like to work with me in the wine shipping department? I have helpers, of course, but it would be wonderful to work with another family member who knows what she's doing."

Rachel was stunned by the offer. "Did you pack the shipment that came to Bella Lucia's?"

"Giles insisted no one else should touch it. How did I do?"

"Every bottle arrived in perfect condition."

"That's a relief. It's a lot of fun really. When we get sore backs we can sit on stools, and if we're nauseated or tired, we'll take time off."

Rachel's gaze swerved to her husband's. "What do you think, Luc?"

He'd just bitten into a peach. She waited for him to swallow.

"I think you should do whatever pleases you."

"But how do you feel about it? Personally, I mean."

He stared at her through shuttered eyes. "Personally I'd love to see you join the family business. It isn't as if you're not used to it. But I'm warning you now. At times we can be as difficult and impossible as anyone within the Valentine organization, so you might not want to make a hard and fast decision today."

"No one could be more difficult than my father. I don't have any reservations about working with Giselle."

Her sister-in-law clapped her hands to her knees. "Then it's settled." She eyed Luc, then Rachel. "I know he wants to keep you all to himself for a few days, so when you're ready, come to th—"

"*Maman?*" One of Giselle's boys was calling to her.

"In the *salon*, Guy."

Rachel turned in time to see Giselle's cute brown-haired sons and husband come in the living room. They must have entered through the basement.

Luc made the introductions. The boys shook Rachel's hand.

"*Bonjour.*"

"*Bonjour.*"

"Speak English to your aunt," Jean-Marc prodded them.

Rachel smiled. "It's all right. I'd rather they helped me with my French."

The youngest boy said, "You and *Maman* don't look *enceinte*."

Rachel knew that word. It meant pregnant.

With a poker face Luc said, "They'll look like swollen grapes by Christmas, Guy."

"Lucien Chartier, what a horrid thing to say!" Giselle chided him, but she said it with a twinkle in her eye.

"By next spring they'll both need a vineyard cart to get around," Jean-Marc heaped it on.

Giselle put her arms around her boys. "Don't listen to them. Just think—next year there will be two new babies in the family."

"Chouette." This from Patrick.

Rachel lifted her head to ask Luc to translate. Her husband read her mind easily. "It means 'cool'."

"It's very *chouette*," Rachel agreed with him.

While they helped themselves to the food, Luc came to stand behind Rachel. He slid his arms around her waist, resting his chin in her hair. "Rachel has agreed to work with Giselle for a while."

Jean-Marc smiled at Rachel. "There's no better vintner to learn from than my wife."

"Were you always a vintner too, Jean-Marc?"

"I worked for another winery in Guebwiller."

"That's not far from Thann," Luc explained. His breath fanned her hair. The sensation made her insides melt.

"One day a package came to the winery meant for Chartier et Fils. The owner told me to deliver it after work. When I walked in the St Hippolyte winery, Giselle was there. We both said hello, and bam, the *coup de foudre* hit me just like that."

Rachel's heart skipped an extra beat. She could relate.

"It didn't hit me quite as fast," Giselle said, getting her own back at her husband.

Everyone smiled except Guy. He looked at his mother with sober eyes and asked her a question in French Rachel couldn't decipher.

"Non, mon fils," Giselle answered, giving him a kiss on the cheek, but it didn't make his worried look go away. At that point Jean-Marc announced they were leaving so the newly-weds could be alone.

With Luc's arm around Rachel's shoulders, they walked Giselle and her family to the front door to see them off.

When their car disappeared below the crest, Rachel looked at her husband whose expression had grown pensive.

"What did Guy ask that made everyone so upset? I heard the verb *mourir* in there somewhere."

Luc breathed in deeply and walked her back to the living room. "He's at the age where he worries about everything."

"Like his mother's baby dying?" Rachel asked.

Luc nodded. "It's more than that. He's afraid the baby will die like Paulette's and mine did, and that will make his *maman* die."

Rachel bowed her head. "That poor child, but I suppose it's only natural when you consider what happened." She eased away without meeting any resistance. It told her a lot about his state of mind.

"Did the doctor know why Paulette lost the baby?"

"Its heart just stopped. He couldn't give us a medical explanation, nor could the autopsy. At a time like that, it was too hard for Paulette to hear the priest say, 'It was God's will'."

"I don't know how you lived through it, Luc." Her voice shook. "Was Paulette working at the time?"

"No. She liked to shop with her friends and occupy herself with home-making hobbies. We went out to dinner often and enjoyed films. The doctor couldn't attribute her lifestyle to the baby's death. It was just one of those things that sometimes happens."

Rachel looked at him. "Are you worried about our baby?"

His dark gaze slid to hers. "Yes. I'll admit I'm terrified."

She bit her lip. "Would you rather I didn't work?"

He raked a hand through his hair. "Until you deliver a healthy baby I'm going to be holding my breath no matter what you do. So I'd rather see you happy doing something I believe you're going to enjoy."

"I know already I'll love working with your sister. I've never been around anyone so effervescent."

He nodded. "Her bright energy infects everyone."

"I like Jean-Marc, too. He seems to be a good match for her. Watching him today I can understand why he'd like to be number one with you."

"Why is that?" She had Luc's full attention now.

"It's obvious Giselle adores you. He wants to measure up in every way."

Luc stroked her cheek with his thumb. "He lit up around you, just like Giles does. You have that effect on men."

"But not on your mother."

His chest rose and fell visibly. "I promise by the time our baby arrives, she'll come around. She's really a wonderful person."

"I know that, Luc. Otherwise you wouldn't be the kind of man you are."

He was the only man Rachel wanted to light up. But for that to happen, she needed to have come into his life before he'd ever met Paulette.

While she stood there wishing she could get his mind off of his sadness for a little while, an idea came to her.

"Wait here. I've got something to show you."

His sensuous mouth lifted at one corner. "Another surprise?"

"In a way."

"If you're after another bottle of wine you've got tucked away, I can save you the trouble. My cellar is fully stocked."

"That's nice to know now that the doctor has taken me off alcohol." While he was still chuckling she added, "Actually I have something else in mind, but it's related."

"Now you've got me curious."

"Good. I'll be right back."

She hurried to the bedroom where she'd noticed her laptop on one of the chairs.

After finding the adapter in her purse, she carried everything back to the kitchen and plugged the cord into the wall outlet behind the bistro table.

She felt Luc's dark eyes watching her. "Come over here. This could take some time."

She set her computer on the tabletop and pulled up the file so he could view the screen.

Luc sat down opposite her. "What's this?"

"Read it and find out."

"'Alsace: God's Vineyard'," he read aloud.

His raised his head. This time when he looked at her, she could tell this was something that had caught his interest. "That's a perfect title. Whose article is this?"

It was a lot more than an article. She'd already written three chapters of a twenty-chapter book she hoped to get published one day. She'd done a mock-up of the pictures she'd already taken to illustrate the passages. There were dozens of photographs that demonstrated everything from the various kinds and sizes of Chartier vineyards to the varieties of grapes that went into their wines. Giles happened to be in several of them.

"Keep on reading and you'll find out."

When she could see he was fully engrossed, she brought the tray in from the living room and cleaned up the kitchen. The whole time she worked, she realized she was holding her breath waiting for his response.

The next time he raised his head, he stared at her as if he'd never seen her before.

"Are you upset with me for the liberties I've taken?" she asked in a nervous voice.

After studying her for a moment, he got up from the table and walked over to her.

His hands went to her shoulders. "On top of everything else, I find I'm married to a writer who has an exceptional grasp of an industry I've worked in all my life. You possess a remarkable gift for combining the technical aspects of wine culture with the ability to express your excitement as only you can do."

A smile broke out on her face. "Thank you."

"It's only the truth. When we first met, one of the qualities I enjoyed most about you was the depth of your appreciation for life. That empathy with the world surrounding you flies off the pages and makes the words live."

His approval meant everything to her. "So you don't mind that you and Giles served as my inspiration?"

His gaze traveled over her upturned features. "You know better than to ask me that question," he murmured. "As I was reading, I marveled to see the thoughts and feelings I've held for years brought to life with such artistry and accuracy.

"Once you've spent some time with Jean-Marc, you can devote a section to Pinot Noir. A good red wine is difficult to achieve. He knows the secret and will be only too happy to tell you all about it."

Luc's unexpected comment thrilled her. She was starting to get really excited about her project.

"I'm hoping that one day when I've finished it, a publisher might be interested." She took an extra breath. "If by some miracle that should happen, would you be willing to write the preface?"

His hands cupped her face. "I'd be honored," he whispered against her lips.

They were leaning against each other, but Luc didn't pull her closer, or try to kiss her the way he'd once done.

Since flying to New York, he was a different person who treated her as if she were an honored guest rather than the love of his life. Since she was neither, she would have settled for something in between.

When she'd agreed to marry him, she'd thought he expected they would sleep together. But he was acting as if he no longer wanted her in that way.

Her heart plunged to her feet. What if he didn't?

She couldn't imagine living with him on a twenty-four-hour basis without the intimacy that had created their baby.

"Your book is such a delight to me, Rachel, I want to return the favor. I haven't furnished the small bedroom off the guest bathroom yet. How would you like to drive into town and we'll start buying some things for a nursery? Anything your heart desires."

Anything her heart desired...

If you didn't love your wife, then the next best thing to do was buy her gifts. But in Rachel's case, everything was for their baby.

She couldn't take exception to that. Her life had been in so much turmoil, she hadn't been able to give a lot of thought to cribs and changing tables yet. But Luc had been through all this before. Though he admitted to being terrified that something could happen to their baby, she sensed he was eager to get busy doing all the fatherly things.

"I'd love it," she said before walking over to the table to get her laptop. "Give me time to change and I'll meet you at the car."

As she started to leave the kitchen she felt his gaze burn through the back of her top.

If she were to turn around now, she had the impression she would see the brooding Luc she'd first met. The man whose moods could change like quicksilver depending on certain situations triggering them.

Was he thinking of the time he and Paulette had picked out a christening cap and gown for their little boy? The joy they'd felt because nothing had yet happened to blot the sun from their universe?

With tears threatening, she ran the rest of the way to the bedroom and went straight for the closet.

Luc had hung up her garment bags. She unzipped one of them and pulled out the white suit she'd worn on her first day in Alsace.

In case they bumped into people he knew while they were in town, she didn't want to let him down.

In an area like this where everyone knew the Chartier name even if they didn't all know him personally, his recent marriage to Rachel was going to create a lot of talk.

Giselle and Jean-Marc's warm welcome had gone a long way to help her handle it. But if by any chance they were to see Luc's in-laws or his mother...

Rachel couldn't think about that right now or she'd have to tell Luc she'd changed her mind about leaving the house.

Once dressed, she removed the ribbon from her hair and brushed it until it swirled against her shoulders.

A touch of lipstick and she felt presentable enough to spend an afternoon out in public with her husband.

Luc's striking coloring and looks made him a target for any woman with eyes to see. Rachel loved him so much she couldn't help but feel a fierce pride to be the woman in his exclusive company.

No one would know she was dying inside for want of the one element needed to make theirs a true marriage.

Somehow she had to present a contented front that would fool Luc into believing everything was all right. But she didn't know how long she could keep it up if he chose to sleep in separate bedrooms tonight.

Luc had just shrugged into his sport jacket when his cell phone rang, the caller ID indicating it was Yves.

By now the news that Luc was married to the pregnant woman he'd gone to see on the same day Paulette had been laid to rest would have reached the Brouets' ears through Luc's mother.

That kind of news would have stretched the limits of friendship with them.

Yves must have run into Jean-Marc or Giselle and knew Luc was back from the States, thus the reason for the call.

Since Rachel would be emerging from the bedroom any minute, Luc stepped out the front door to talk to him in private.

Once they were seen buying baby furniture in Ribeauville, word of their marriage would spread to the four corners of Alsace. In the days to come after a routine had been established, it was inevitable Rachel would run into certain people who would shun her out of loyalty to Paulette. Luc wouldn't always be at her side to protect her.

He clicked on and said hello.

"Is it true you're married to Rachel Valentine, and expecting a baby, and you didn't tell me first?"

Luc bowed his head. "We just got back from New York last night."

"Do you have any idea how long I've prayed for someone to come along and sweep you off your feet? Giles told me how valiant you were trying to fight your attraction to Rachel, but he said the *coup de foudre* hit you so hard, both of you went around in a daze that was fascinating to watch."

Those words unlocked the vise holding Luc in its grip. Too much emotion made it difficult to talk for a minute.

"Camille and I want to meet her. How about bringing her over to the house for dinner tonight? I don't think I can wait any longer. Giles says she's a real beauty."

"She is," Luc whispered in a thick-toned voice as his wife stepped out on the porch wearing the white suit he loved. The heart-stopping memory of her sitting in the hotel dining room savoring the Tokay would stay with him all his days.

"Just a second and I'll check with her."

"Who is it?" she mouthed the words nervously.

The day Rachel no longer had to worry about being accepted

couldn't come soon enough for Luc. Yves' phone call was a giant step in the right direction.

He cupped her neck and whispered into her ear. "Yves. He and Camille have invited us for a celebration dinner at their house this evening. Would you like to do that after we're through shopping?"

When he sensed her hesitation he added, "He called us, not the other way around. It means he's happy for us and wants the four of us to start doing things together. No man ever had a better friend."

He felt the fortifying breath she took. "Under the circumstances, he must be exceptional."

"He is."

"Of course I want to go if you do."

He kissed her soft cheek, then spoke into the phone again. "We'd love to come, Yves. What time?"

"Camille says any time after six."

"We'll be there. *Merci, mon ami.*"

CHAPTER ELEVEN

WHILE the men were outside with the children, Rachel helped Camille do the dishes.

Rachel knew there would be times when Luc needed to talk about Paulette. Who better than with her brother Yves? Rachel would give her husband all the space he needed.

As for Camille, Rachel had felt an instant rapport with her. She reminded her of Emma. Sweet and unpretentious.

"You're a fabulous cook like my half sister, who's the head chef at Bella Lucia. Thank you for going to all this trouble for us."

"It was our pleasure, believe me. Luc is family. It's been hard to see how empty his life has been over the last three years. But now I know the reason."

"What do you mean?"

"He clearly had to wait until your grandfather asked you to come to Alsace so you and he could meet. It was all part of a grand design, but I didn't realize it before tonight."

Her eyes smiled at Rachel. "You're wonderful for Luc. That book you're writing on wines shows you value not only him, but the work he does. Not every woman makes a good vintner's wife."

Was Camille telling her something about Paulette? Rachel didn't dare ask. Instead she put the dried plates away in the cupboard.

"If I were you, I know I'd be riddled with curiosity about Paulette," Camille confided. "But since you're too polite to bring her name up, then let me."

She smiled at Rachel. "She was blond like Yves, fun and full of life like he is. If you know Yves, you know Paulette."

Since Rachel was already crazy about Yves, who kept them all laughing, she could understand how Luc would have adored his sister.

"I understand they knew each other for years."

"Yes, and from an early age Paulette set her sights on Luc. In that respect she wasn't any different from all the other females around who considered Lucien Chartier the catch of all time."

He still was…

"Instead of going away to college, she stayed in St Hippolyte to break Luc down and get in his face until he married her. Her goal in life was to be his wife and have his children."

The two women stared at each other before Rachel said, "Not every dream works out exactly as we want, does it? My twin sister Rebecca suffers from endometriosis. I know she's frightened she can't have children. It's very sad."

"Life is strange," Camille murmured. "I was a schoolteacher and wanted a few years alone with Yves before children came along, but they came anyway. Not that I'm complaining, you understand." She laughed gently.

"I—I'm afraid I never gave it a great deal of thought until I discovered I was pregnant," Rachel confessed. "For the first month I was in total shock, but after today I must admit I'm getting excited."

"Lucky you to be married to a man who can't wait for the big event. It looks like he bought out the stores this afternoon."

"As you saw from everything, we went overboard."

"Why not? Luc's going to make a terrific father."

"I'm sure of it. But my heart still breaks when I think of the pain he and Paulette went through losing their baby." Her voice trembled.

"Any miscarriage is a terrible loss. I had one between my son and daughter."

"Luc told me. I'm so sorry."

"It's all right, Rachel, and it should have been all right for

Paulette because the doctor told her there was no reason why she couldn't try again.

"I truly believe that if she'd had more going on in her life so she didn't obsess over getting pregnant, she wouldn't have gone off the deep end after she miscarried."

"Was it postpartum depression?"

"That too—however, Yves and I think Paulette had a chemical imbalance. The problem was, she refused to see a psychiatrist so she didn't get the help she needed.

"Her paranoia got so bad she accused Luc of not loving her anymore because she couldn't produce his baby. It made no sense. He would have done anything and told her they could adopt. But she wouldn't hear of it. It had to be Luc's baby or nothing. She simply wasn't rational about it."

Rachel shivered. "He said she pushed him away."

"It's true. When she asked for the divorce, we all realized how sick she was. Everyone loved Paulette, but she needed professional help to get past her grief. Not even Yves' parents could get her to consider it."

"How tragic."

Camille patted her arm. "It's over now. Luc has put it behind him. You need to do the same thing."

When Rachel started to protest Camille said, "I know. It's easier said than done. If I could give you one piece of advice whether you want it or not, don't hold anything back from Luc. Not your fears or your concerns. Talk to him. Tell him what you're thinking and feeling. Don't shut him out the way she did.

"Paulette's mental state put him in a straightjacket. A marriage like that can't survive under those conditions."

"I'm sure you're right. Thank you." She hugged Camille before they walked through the house. It sounded as if the men had come in with the children.

Rachel would take Camille's advice, but she feared her marriage wouldn't survive despite Luc's determination to make it work. He wasn't in love with her. It was that simple.

As she entered the living room his brown eyes cast her a speculative glance.

"You look tired. After the full day we've put in, I'm not surprised. I think it's time to get you home to bed."

She didn't feel in the least tired, but her heart pounded against her ribs to think he might desire her enough to want their honeymoon to begin tonight.

"Come on, everyone." Yves spoke to his family. "Let's help take out all these baby things to Luc's car."

"Thank you for the dinner, and the mobile," Rachel said a few minutes later, giving Camille and Yves another hug.

"We'll have you over for dinner next weekend," Luc said before helping Rachel into the front seat of the Wagoneer.

"A bientôt."

During the drive home, Rachel turned to him. "They're lovely people. I never expected such a warm welcome."

"They like you."

"Because of you."

She smiled. "My grandfather used to say you can judge a man's character by his closest friend. Yves is a choice person. So is his wife."

He reached for her hand and squeezed it. "After spending the evening with you, they genuinely want to be your friend."

His gaze searched hers. "What did you and Camille talk about so long in the kitchen?"

Rachel had already made up her mind to follow the other woman's advice. "Paulette."

Slowly he let go of her hand and put his back on the steering wheel.

"I suppose that was inevitable. You can ask me anything you want about her, Rachel."

"I know that. Camille was the one who offered information she suspected I'd like to know."

"Did you learn anything new?"

"Only that Paulette was fun-loving like Yves."

"Once upon a time she was."

Luc's honesty was another quality she admired. But this was one time when the truth was like a bullet wound straight through the heart.

"Is there anything else you want to know about Paulette before we close the book on her?" he asked, sounding so remote all of a sudden, she didn't know how to reach him.

Rachel took a shuddering breath. "Can *you*? Close the book, I mean?"

"It closed when I saw the vacant look in her eyes and realized that her spirit had gone."

With those words spoken, there was nothing more to be said. Desolate, Rachel stared out the passenger window. They drove the rest of the way to the house in tension-filled silence. The kind that made her feel worlds apart from him though their bodies were almost touching.

The moment they pulled in front of the garage, Luc jumped out and came around to let her inside the house.

He'd put his hand on the back of her neck to guide her. "You go ahead and get ready for bed. I'll bring in the baby's things."

She had an idea that if she argued with him by insisting she help, he would go all forbidding on her.

Being an expectant father for a second time made him feel a deeper sense of responsibility for her than normal. She couldn't fault him for it, but she'd never been treated like a piece of prized porcelain before.

So far her pregnancy had gone well. She hadn't experienced any morning sickness. According to what she'd learned from Luc, Paulette's pregnancy had seemed routine up to the moment the doctor had told her the baby was no longer alive.

Paulette again.

Rachel needed to stop thinking about her, but how?

After a quick shower, she put on a nightgown and climbed into bed. She could hear Luc down the hall bringing more things in from the car.

He was taking so long, she finally switched off the lamp while she waited for him in the darkness. But after a half-hour, she gave up hope that he had any intention of joining her.

In excruciating pain, Rachel turned over and buried her wet face in the pillow.

At some point she must have gone to sleep. She didn't realize it until something disturbed her. Once again she woke up to discover she was alone in Luc's bed. Her watch said nine-thirty in the morning.

The house was quiet. It meant Luc had gone to bed downstairs.

She threw back the covers to put on her robe and sandals. Without hesitation she stole down the hall. The second she saw the assembled crib in the nursery, her heart melted to think he'd spent part of last night putting it together.

Needing to talk to him, she went down the stairs to see if he was up yet. If so, she would fix him breakfast.

The moment she reached the storage room, she noticed the door to the vineyard was ajar, letting in light.

She poked her head outside and saw his well-honed frame hunkered down in the vines on the lower slope.

Whether in a sport jacket or jeans and navy T-shirt as he was wearing this morning, he took her breath away.

She walked outside and made her way carefully between the rows to catch up to him.

"Luc?" she called his name in a quiet voice.

He stood up abruptly and wheeled around. "Rachel—what's wrong?"

Why did anything have to be wrong?

"Nothing. I just came out to find you and say good morning."

The blood had actually started to drain from his face. There was a look of fear in his eyes, causing her heart to twist in pain because he was so anxious.

He raked an unsteady hand through his hair. "*Ma chérie*, you're all right." His eyes scrutinized her relentlessly.

Like the day of the storm, he was so upset she was beginning to understand just how much this baby meant to him.

She rubbed her palms against her hips nervously. His gaze took in the telling gesture.

"I looked in the nursery. You did a fabulous job putting the crib together. It looks beautiful in there."

He didn't say anything. She babbled on. "I'm glad we picked the walnut. Our baby's going to be very happy. But you could have waited until today to do it. After a late night, how come you're up so early? You need your sleep, too."

He glanced out over the landscape. "Insomnia has plagued me for a long time. I'm sorry if my movements disturbed you. You need your rest."

All she needed was her husband's love. But his mind was so far removed from being with her, let alone making love to her, she was shattered.

"You're right, Luc. The more rest, the better for the baby. But I got a good sleep and am up now. Would you like breakfast?"

"Thank you, but I'm not hungry this morning. I'll come in later and fix lunch for us."

Making a snap decision, she said, "I won't be here for lunch, but I'll make it for you before I go."

His dark gaze flew to hers once more. "Go where?"

"To the winery. I'm meeting with Giselle. Which car do you want me to take?"

Her question appeared to have caught him off guard. If anything, he looked more ashen faced.

"You want to start work today?" He sounded incredulous.

"Like you, I'm somewhat of a workaholic."

His mouth thinned. "If that's what you want, then I'll drive you." He started walking toward her.

"That won't be necessary. You're busy doing your work. I need to be able to drive to mine."

"I sold the Maserati and need to buy you a car. For the time being, I'll take you," he declared in a tone of finality. "If you leave in the Wagoneer and were to get into trouble, I wouldn't be able to help you."

Rachel was confused. "Why did you sell it?"

He pursed his lips. "Now that we're a family, it's not safe or practical."

"But you didn't know we were going to be a family until a week ago. What made you sell it?"

"It was Paulette's. I arranged for it to be sold the day after she died."

"I see." Rachel could understand how hard it would have been for him to keep something like that of hers around.

She turned to go back in the basement, then paused. "Your mother said you'd built this house in the hope that when Paulette woke up, she would start a new life with you here.

"If you want to sell the house, but were afraid to broach the subject with me, it's all right, Luc."

She'd almost made it to the door when she sensed him close behind her.

"Mother was wrong about that, Rachel. I didn't start building this house until eight months ago. She assumed it was for Paulette. In reality, I built it for me."

What?

Rachel's hand clung to the door handle.

"*Maman* was getting too used to my living with her and Giselle's family. I only stayed in her house as long as I did because she had a bad time of it after *Papa* died and my being there seemed to help her cope better, but there came a time when I realized I needed to be on my own again.

"As for the car, it was the one Paulette was driving the day of the accident."

Oh, no.

Rachel shook her head. "When I think what terrible things I said to you about not wanting to ride in it with you—"

"You were preaching to the converted," he murmured. "I'm glad it's gone. I had the repairs done because everyone assumed she would come out of her coma within days or weeks, and kept the car with me as her family couldn't bear the sight of it. The few times you saw me driving it, I was making sure it stayed in good running condition."

He shifted his weight. "Why don't we buy you a Wagoneer like mine? It'll be safe for you and the baby. Plus you'll find it convenient when you take future clients on tours of the vineyards at odd hours."

Rachel was incredulous. "You want me to do that?"

"Of course. It wasn't something Paulette could or would do. She didn't know that much about my work, and showed little interest in it. You on the other hand are going to be one of Domaine Chartier's greatest assets."

Luc could hear her mind working back to the night they had first met.

"Then—"

"I lied that night," he cut in on her. Those gorgeous dark-fringed blue eyes widened in astonishment. "I wanted to be with you, and I refused to take no for an answer. But I didn't want to frighten you off, so I made up the part about my ex-wife normally doing the honors. I hoped it would reassure you. Does that shock you?"

Her expression was a picture of bewilderment.

"Don't you mean you didn't want to lose a possible sale?"

"No," he whispered. Unable to hold off any longer, he gripped her arms covered by her silky pink robe. "I didn't care about anything except making sure you didn't get away from me."

Her eyes looked wounded. "You don't have to say that, Luc. I know how you felt about Paulette. How you still feel…"

"Listen to me." He shook her gently. "I loved her. We got married and had some wonderful years together, but everything came apart before we were actually divorced.

"Until I laid eyes on you coming around the bend in the road, I didn't know how over our marriage I really was.

"Out of the blue came this knockout woman driving toward me. The truth is, I almost ran into you because I was so attracted, every other thought went out of my head."

She eyed him soulfully, as if measuring the veracity of his words.

"I'd memorized your license-plate number and intended to track you down. Then a miracle occurred because there you were, sitting in the Hotel du Roi dining room drinking *my* wine."

He smiled. "Right then I made up my mind I had to have you no matter how long it took, or what I had to do."

Rachel's body tingled as he pulled her closer. "I swear to you Paulette didn't figure in my consciousness. All I could think of was how to get you into my arms. You were the most beautiful sight I'd ever seen.

"I wanted to kidnap you that night. You have no idea the

will-power it took to put Giles in charge of you. But I crumbled the next morning, and that night, and the next day and night."

He kissed her astonished mouth. "My feelings for you were so intense, I was terrified I'd frighten you off.

"When the storm came up and you offered to help me tie my vines, I couldn't get you to my house fast enough. Do you understand what I'm telling you? I fell in love with *you*, Rachel Chartier. Completely, irrevocably. It happened so fast, I'm still reeling.

"It happened that night in the vineyard. You took over my heart. I wanted you in my bed, in my life for ever."

"Luc—"

"It's true, *mon amour*. The morning after we made love, I planned to tell you everything about Paulette before I asked you to marry me. But you were still asleep so I slipped out early to drive to Thann."

"Thann?"

"I couldn't propose to you without a certain necessary item." She looked stunned. "You mean the nuptial jug?"

"Yes."

"But if you'd already drunk from it with Paulette, I—"

"Rachel—that jug never left the *armoire* until I went for it the morning after we made love. You see, I never officially proposed to Paulette."

"You didn't?" she asked tentatively.

"No. One day Yves said, 'You two should get married or never see each other again.' That was it."

"But your mother said you went to the hospital, and—"

"*Maman* said a lot of things without knowing the truth of the situation."

He kissed her throat. "When are you going to start listening to me? I was so madly in love with you, Paulette wasn't in my thoughts.

"Shh." He quieted her with his lips as she started to protest again. "*Maman* was projecting her own feelings about *Papa* and hasn't been through a divorce to understand how my failed marriage killed my feelings for Paulette. Happily married couples can't comprehend what it's like, and I swear to you that the only thing driving me for the last few years has been…guilt."

She shook her head in bewilderment. "Why guilt? You didn't do anything wrong," she declared passionately.

He drew in a sharp breath. "I thought I did."

"What do you mean?"

"When Paulette and I separated, I told you I moved back into my parents' home so she could still live in the house I bought for us.

"Two days after the judge granted the divorce, Paulette phoned me about the deed to the house I'd given her in the decree. She wanted it to give to her attorney, and asked me to bring it to her, but I suggested she come by the office because I was too busy.

"There was a terrible storm that day, the kind you and I got caught in last month, and during the downpour the truck skidded into her car and knocked her unconscious. If I'd dropped what I was doing and had gone to her, she would still be alive and able to work out her future."

Rachel cupped his face. "You couldn't have known that truck would run into her. That wasn't your fault!"

He kissed her hands. "I know that now. But all those feelings and fears got twisted for a long time. Once I heard about the accident, I didn't cease begging her forgiveness. But I could never be sure if she heard me.

"I knew that once her family made the decision to turn off the machines, there wouldn't be a possibility of her hearing me, let alone forgiving me."

He smiled sadly. "That's why I was determined she would wake up. That had been my torture until you told me about your twin, and I saw what guilt did to you for something that wasn't your fault. You helped me understand how wrong it was to keep punishing myself. That's when I let go of my guilt."

"Oh, Luc—" She threw her arms around his neck. "You poor darling. So *that's* the reason you were so upset when you carried me in the house during the storm. You kept saying it was your fault because we'd worked outside too long. I couldn't understand your suffering."

He pressed his forehead to hers. "The thought of anything happening to you almost paralyzed me and you know why, don't you? I love you, Rachel Chartier, and I believe you love me. But I've never heard you say the words. Tell me you love me," he begged.

"I *have* told you—" she cried. "Over and over again. Why do you think I married you? It was for one reason only. I'm in love with you!

"When I told you that you were the only man I ever wanted, I was really telling you I'd fallen head over heels in love. But I didn't know your true feelings."

He crushed her mouth with his own, drowning in euphoria because she was kissing him back with the whole of her heart and soul.

His mother's words filled his mind.

If you could have heard the joy in her voice, or have seen the stars in her eyes...

Luc was hearing and seeing and feeling it all now...

He bound her soft, curving warmth to him.

"When I came to your hotel room in Colmar and you told me I'd made you pregnant, I learned the meaning of joy, and vowed I'd never let you out of my sight again.

"Because of my past history with Paulette, I wanted to give you time to accept the fact that I was in love with you. Staying away from you every night has been an agony I never want to go through again."

"Neither do I!"

"You have to forgive me for going about everything the wrong way, Rachel. If you hadn't come back to Alsace, I would have tracked you down in New York the next day."

She covered his face with kisses. "I'll forgive you for everything on one condition."

His breath caught. "Anything."

"Take me in the house and propose to me in the time-honored Chartier way. If we have a son, then I want to be able to tell him that's how his father made our marriage official."

* * *

Hours later Rachel stirred in her husband's arms. He was finally out for the count.

She smiled, unable to move because their legs were entwined and his arm was fastened possessively around her hips.

At last she knew he was madly in love with her and wanted only her for ever.

They hadn't been able to get enough of each other.

So much the better since they had the rest of their lives stretching before them to shower each other with that love.

She looked over at the ancient green jug sitting on the end table.

"The marriage ritual of the vine," Luc had called it, while his eyes had blazed with adoration.

Rachel gave a great sigh of contentment and nestled closer to her impossibly handsome French prince.

Somehow she had the feeling her grandfather knew she'd found her great happiness.

If she and Luc had a son, how she'd love to call him Guillaume Valentine Chartier. She'd already decided on the name Rebecca if they had a girl.

Of course Luc would have to approve of her choices.

Impatient to know his thoughts on the subject, she kissed him with growing hunger to bring him awake.

"I've been waiting for you," he murmured feverishly. Though his gorgeous brown eyes were still closed, he responded with breathtaking ardor.

Rachel realized it was going to be a while before she had her answers.

But it didn't matter. She'd come home to God's garden with her husband. They had all the time in the world…

* * * * *

The next book in THE BRIDES OF BELLA LUCIA *series
is out next month!*
Don't miss THE REBEL PRINCE *by Raye Morgan*

Here's an exclusive sneak preview of Emma Valentine's story!

"OH, NO!"

The reaction slipped out before Emma Valentine could stop it, for there stood the very man she most wanted to avoid seeing again.

He didn't look any happier to see her.

"Well, come on, get on board," he said gruffly. "I won't bite." One eyebrow rose. "Though I might nibble a little," he added, mostly to amuse himself.

But she wasn't paying any attention to what he was saying. She was staring at him, taking in the royal blue uniform he was wearing, with gold braid and glistening badges decorating the sleeves, epaulettes and an upright collar. Ribbons and medals covered the breast of the short, fitted jacket. A gold-encrusted sabre hung at his side. And suddenly it was clear to her who this man really was.

She gulped wordlessly. Reaching out, he took her elbow and pulled her aboard. The doors slid closed. And finally she found her tongue.

"You…you're the prince."

He nodded, barely glancing at her. "Yes. Of course."

She raised a hand and covered her mouth for a moment. "I should have known."

"Of course you should have. I don't know why you didn't." He punched the ground-floor button to get the elevator moving again, then turned to look down at her. "A relatively bright five-year-old child would have tumbled to the truth right away."

Her shock faded as her indignation at his tone asserted itself. He might be the prince, but he was still just as annoying as he had been earlier that day.

"A relatively bright five-year-old child without a bump on the head from a badly thrown water polo ball, maybe," she said defensively. She wasn't feeling woozy any longer and she wasn't about to let him bully her, no matter how royal he was. "I was unconscious half the time."

"And just clueless the other half, I guess," he said, looking bemused.

The arrogance of the man was really galling.

"I suppose you think your 'royalness' is so obvious it sort of shimmers around you for all to see?" she challenged. "Or better yet, oozes from your pores like…like sweat on a hot day?"

"Something like that," he acknowledged calmly. "Most people tumble to it pretty quickly. In fact, it's hard to hide even when I want to avoid dealing with it."

"Poor baby," she said, still resenting his manner. "I guess that works better with injured people who are half asleep." Looking at him, she felt a strange emotion she couldn't identify. It was as though she wanted to prove something to him, but she wasn't sure what. "And anyway, you know you did your best to fool me," she added.

His brows knit together as though he really didn't know what she was talking about. "I didn't do a thing."

"You told me your name was Monty."

"It is." He shrugged. "I have a lot of names. Some of them are too rude to be spoken to my face, I'm sure." He glanced at her sideways, his hand on the hilt of his sabre. "Perhaps you're contemplating one of those right now."

You bet I am.

That was what she would like to say. But it suddenly occurred to her that she was supposed to be working for this man. If she wanted to keep the job of coronation chef, maybe she'd better keep her opinions to herself. So she clamped her mouth shut, took a deep breath and looked away, trying hard to calm down.

The elevator ground to a halt and the doors slid open laboriously. She moved to step forward, hoping to make her escape, but his hand shot out again and caught her elbow.

"Wait a minute. *You're* a woman," he said, as though that thought had just presented itself to him.

"That's a rare ability for insight you have there, Your Highness," she snapped before she could stop herself. And then she winced. She was going to have to do better than that if she was going to keep this relationship on an even keel.

But he was ignoring her dig. Nodding, he stared at her with a speculative gleam in his golden eyes. "I've been looking for a woman, but you'll do."

She blanched, stiffening. "I'll do for what?"

He made a head gesture in a direction she knew was opposite of where she was going and his grip tightened on her elbow.

"Come with me," he said abruptly, making it an order.

She dug in her heels, thinking fast. She didn't much like orders. "Wait! I can't. I have to get to the kitchen."

"Not yet. I need you."

"You what?" Her breathless gasp of surprise was soft, but she knew he'd heard it.

"I need you," he said firmly. "Oh, don't look so shocked. I'm not planning to throw you into the hay and have my way with you. I need you for something a bit more mundane than that."

She felt color rushing into her cheeks and she silently begged it to stop. Here she was, formless and stodgy in her chef's whites. No makeup, no stiletto heels. Hardly the picture of the femmes fatales he was undoubtedly used to. The likelihood that he would have any carnal interest in her was remote at best. To have him think she was hysterically defending her virtue was humiliating.

"Well, what if I don't want to go with you?" she said in hopes of deflecting his attention from her blush.

"Too bad."

"What?"

Amusement sparkled in his eyes. He was certainly enjoying this. And that only made her more determined to resist him.

"I'm the prince, remember? And we're in the castle. My orders take precedence. It's that old pesky divine rights thing."

Her jaw jutted out. Despite her embarrassment, she couldn't let that pass.

"Over my free will? Never!"

Exasperation filled his face.

"Hey, call out the historians. Someone will write a book about you and your courageous principles." His eyes glittered sardonically. "But in the meantime, Emma Valentine, you're coming with me."

Page-turning drama...

Exotic, glamorous locations...

Intense emotion and passionate seduction...

Sheikhs, princes and billionaire tycoons...

This summer, may we suggest:

THE SHEIKH'S DISOBEDIENT BRIDE
by Jane Porter

On sale June.

AT THE GREEK TYCOON'S BIDDING
by Cathy Williams

On sale July.

THE ITALIAN MILLIONAIRE'S VIRGIN WIFE

On sale August.

With new titles to choose from every month,
discover a world of romance in our books written
by internationally bestselling authors.

It's the ultimate in quality romance!

Available wherever Harlequin books are sold.

www.eHarlequin.com

HPGEN06